Voices Unheard and Lessons Learned

KHETAM DAHI

Illustrated by: Novia Elvina

authorHOUSE®

AuthorHouse™
1663 Liberty Drive
Bloomington, IN 47403
www.authorhouse.com
Phone: 1 (800) 839-8640

Interior Graphics/Art Credit: Novia Elvina

Published by AuthorHouse 03/12/2019

ISBN: 978-1-7283-0368-0 (sc)
ISBN: 978-1-7283-0367-3 (e)

Print information available on the last page.

This book is printed on acid-free paper.

Dedication

To my students and friends

Acknowledgements

I would like to thank all my students and friends who have shared their own inspirational stories with me throughout the years. They are the reason I wanted to write the stories in this book. I also want to thank my husband Ayham Dahi and our kids, Reem, Jamal and Joel for their feedback and for their constant support and encouragement in every project I take on.

Contents

Evie from Casillas, Guatemala: A Hellish Journey

"I should have let your mommy abort you when she had the chance." My aunt, Sonia used to say to me when I gave her a hard time. She was managing a dirty **brothel** in the small town of Casillas. It was a municipality in Santa Rosa department of south-west Guatemala.

My aunt's business was located in a run-down neighborhood and it was a house that was owned by a local **pimp**. They say that he had killed two ex-wives within a three-year period but was never found guilty for either crime. He made enough money off the backs of the women working for him that people used to say he may have **bribed** the police and the judge in town to drop the cases.

How did I end up in the brothel? Well, my mother, according to my aunt and grandmother, had died when I was three years old and my younger brother was one. Over the years, though, I heard many stories from people in the neighborhood that my mother was still alive but had run away with a man.

Since my mother didn't know who our fathers were, I was sent to live with my aunt, and my brother stayed with my maternal grandmother, who was already taking care of three other grandchildren. Their mother had left them behind and came to Arizona to work. She was my aunt, Mara, my mother's older sister.

From the day I arrived at the brothel at the age of three, Aunt Sonia started **mistreating** and **abusing** me. To begin with, I had to sleep in a very small and dirty room in the back of the brothel where I was abandoned most of the day. I basically fed myself and ran around the house looking for any attention, even from strangers. Sometimes when my aunt noticed me, she would hug me for a second and then tell me to go back to my room.

By the time I was eight years old, I had to clean the house, wash the clothes by hand and hang them out on the line to dry. I also had to cook dinner for at least ten women and some of their children every night. My aunt would take money from their daily wages to pay for the food. Some of the women were afraid they would not be able to eat at home because their husbands took all the money and spent most of it on their drinking habit. It was a lot easier to eat and feed their little ones at the brothel before they went home.

After everyone left the brothel every evening, I was then able to do my homework. I actually loved going to school because I was away from the **disgustingly revolting** atmosphere at home. The overwhelming smell of incense was nauseating, and men used to come and go all day and all night.

There were smelly men, ugly men, old men, rich men who didn't want to be recognized in their own circles, drunk men, and even poor men who borrowed or stole money to pay for sex. The women who worked there were very poor, and some of them were married and had kids.

I knew a woman who brought her daughter with her to work every day, and I used to babysit her. She was only seven years old but thought beyond her years.

"Maybe one day I will work here, too." She would tell me.

"Don't be stupid!" I would yell. "These women are selling their bodies and getting abused."

"Yes, but they are making money. My mom makes enough money to pay for everything in the house. My dad is always drunk, and if she doesn't work, we don't eat." She would say.

I did not want that to be an option for me. So, while living with my aunt, I was planning to escape every single day. I played different scenarios in my head and plan the whole thing out and study it from many angles, and if there was any chance of my getting caught, I would tell myself, *"I will plan something else tomorrow."*

I would constantly rattle my brain for new ideas to leave the brothel and go somewhere else. I always ended up asking myself, *"How will I live? Who would pay for my food and* **shelter***? How would I be able to go to school?"* the bottom line was that something always hindered me from leaving or life's daily routine **derailed** me from accomplishing my dream.

The days and the years went by, and I was now fourteen years old. Men were already looking at me as **vultures** look at their next **prey** before attacking. I was scared of being assaulted every minute of the day and even more scared that my classmates would finally find out where I lived. The worst part about this was that I did not feel protected by my aunt. It was as if she was just waiting for me to be of age to join her in the business.

One day after I had talked to some people in town, I found out that I could cross the border to Mexico and from there, I could try to come to Arizona, if everything went as planned.

I called my other aunt, Mara and told her that I could no longer live in the brothel and that I wanted to come to the states and stay with her.

"I could help you in the house with whatever you need if you pay the **"coyotes"** *the money I would owe."* I proposed.

We went back and forth in the conversation and discussed many options, but she finally and **miraculously** said yes to my proposal.

Two weeks later, I packed all my things. I hid my backpack outside in the yard, behind the bushes. I woke up early that day as to go to school, got ready, made breakfast for everyone, cleaned the kitchen and left the house.

I walked through the side streets and alleys so that nobody I knew would see me. Then, I rode the bus from Casillas, which took me to a small town near Tucuman, a municipality of Palenque in Mexico in the State of Chiapas.

The coyotes were there waiting for the group of 40 people. I walked over and joined the crowd that was standing to the right of road and asked, *"Is this where we wait to cross the border?"*

A lady said, "Yes, just make sure you stand next to your parents."

"I am by myself." I told her quietly.

"Then, come over here and stay close to us." She grabbed my hand tightly.

We all got into the back of a huge truck. We were literally stacked on top of each other like sardines. Two heavy women sitting in my lap.

We drove for four hours, stopping here and there for drivers to switch. We arrived in a small town called, Tapachula (the name means between the waters), another municipality in the State of Chiapas near the Guatemalan border.

All the way there, we had no food or drinks so that we wouldn't need to go to the bathroom. At some point, I didn't have any feeling in my legs. Somehow, we all just sat there without saying a word to each other. I think the heavy weight finally made me tired and I fell asleep for a while.

When the coyotes opened the back door to the truck, people **stormed out**. It took me a few minutes to actually feel my legs to be able to stand up.

"Get out, girl! What are you waiting for?" A man yelled.

We were taken to a **barn** nearby in the town of Chiapas, Mexico to get new ID cards with different names.

Then, we boarded a bus, and this time, we each had our own seat. Still, we had no water, but were given some dried food to be able to **survive** the rest of the way.

The bus ride lasted 24 hours, as we left early in the morning from Chiapas and arrived in Puebla, a Spanish colonial city in Mexico, the following morning.

We rested for a while and used the bathroom (a tiny place for which I had to wait an hour to be able to go into).

Then we were back in an eighteen-wheeler truck, stacked on top of each other again like chickens ready to be slaughtered. The back of the truck had many boxes full of different **merchandize**, which were used to line the sides and the back of the crate. The driver did this so that if he were pulled over, the police would see only boxes.

We were also given a few **axes** to use in case of losing air. The idea was to use the axes to open holes in the wall of the truck, but only in very extreme circumstances, like if someone was **suffocating**.

On the way there, this time, I was able to talk to some people and make some friends. We shared stories and even managed to laugh a bit about silly things, mostly related to how we ended up on this journey.

A lady who sat near me was very annoyed why I was laughing. She was **judgmental** and stared at me with dirty looks on her face.

"You're not going to make it, little girl. You are a trouble maker and you are making this very difficult for all of us." She discouraged me. "You're laughing with guys like a whore." She added.

I just ignored her. I thought that soon, I would get to my destination and would not have to deal with her anymore.

The journey lasted three days and three nights. We then arrived in Mexico City.

The guides took us to a motel where we received food and water. We stayed there for three nights. I continued to talk and laugh with a couple of guys who were with us on the truck. Then, another young man joined us. He was one of the guides.

We ate together in the courtyard of the small motel. The lady who was annoyed by me was looking at us from afar, making faces at me, in particular. I still ignored her and kept having fun with the guys.

The coyotes woke us up very early the next day. It was still dark, but they told us we had to walk to Altar, a small town in the state of Sonora, Mexico and bordering Arizona, U.S.A.

I noticed that our group got a lot smaller. Some people had gone with another group of coyotes. I found myself the only female in my group. We walked all night in the desert without food or water. We slept wherever we could find some shelter behind trees.

Once we arrived in Arizona, different coyotes took over my group. They were supposed to deliver me to my aunt's house in Phoenix. One of the previous coyotes told me to be careful before he let me go with the new group. There were finally four guys and I plus the three coyotes. We kept walking in the Arizona desert, stopping along the way to rest. At night, we had to sleep for a few hours to be able to walk the rest of the way to get to the other coyotes.

As I tried to find a good spot to sleep, one of the guides came and whispered, "I need to protect you from the other men. So, you come with me."

I didn't feel comfortable with him. He looked and sounded kind of creepy.

"What do you mean? Aren't you all supposed to protect us together?" I asked **confusingly.**

"Yes, but you never know what can happen with these guys' heads sometimes. They can get lonely on these long journeys. I have seen all kinds of things happen to girls like you. You don't want to be one of those cases." He said in a dim voice.

He took my hand and led me behind a tree away from the other groups.

"Here you go. We'll sleep here until dawn and then we will continue our journey." He placed a blanket on the ground and asked me to sleep there.

It was a bit cold, and I only had my jacket. I put the hood over my head and tried to sleep. Suddenly, I felt the guy's body moving close to me. I acted as if I did not see him, but my eyes were half shut. I saw a look on him like the one you see when a lion is getting ready to attack its prey- like the men I used to see at the brothel.

He slowly crept up and put his arm around me.

"It's OK little girl. I'm only here to protect you."

He then put his hand over my mouth and held my body down tight.

"Do not say a word, you hear?" He **threatened** me with a knife in his other hand.

I must have blacked out for a while because I woke up to find myself bleeding and half my clothes were off. I looked across the way and saw everyone sleeping. Jesus, the attacker, was also sleeping next to the other guys as if nothing had happened.

I gathered myself and tried to clean up. I threw my head back against the tree **stump** and thought I could sleep a little, but I was too scared to fall asleep. It was still dark.

"What if the other guys decided to have their way with me?" I fearfully wondered. Jesus had told me that I never know what these guys would do.

I stayed up all night, and when the guys woke up, I was already set to continue walking. After walking in the heat for a few hours, we arrived at the **pre-determined** destination where a driver was going to take me to my aunt's house in Phoenix.

We drove for a couple of hours with one stop for gas and a bathroom break. The driver and I never said a word to each other. It was very obvious that I had been assaulted. My mouth was swollen, and I had a black nose. In retrospect, I know that he had some idea of what had taken place back in the woods. But, he continued driving and was completely silent the whole way.

When I got to the front door of my aunt's house, the driver followed me in order to receive the rest of the money we owed the coyotes. My aunt hugged me and asked me what happened to my face.

"What the Hell did you do to my niece? Who hurt her? Somebody is going to pay for this." She yelled at the driver.

For the first few days of my staying with my aunt, she was nice, but gradually, she started assigning me some work around the house. The work load increased every day, and her attitude toward me became very negative and sometimes **hostile**. After two months, I realized I may be pregnant, because I was feeling tired and **nauseous** and looked very pale.

I had already told my aunt that I had been attacked by one of the coyotes, but I did not tell her that he had raped me. Now, I had to tell her that, and that I was pregnant, which was going to make things between us a lot worse.

A couple of days later, Aunt Mara took me to a local walk-in clinic, and the test came out positive. She was **furious** with me and started calling me names, like whore and prostitute. I was back at square one. This is exactly what I did not to be called or become. By this time, my cousin, Gloria, Aunt Sonia's daughter, had been asking me to live with her, but I kept **refusing**.

So, when things became **unbearable** in my aunt's house, I decided to move in with Gloria. She had three kids, but their father was not living with them. I thought it would be great to stay together and bond while helping each other.

That was not how things worked out, though. Instead, Gloria **subjected** me to all types of hard labor work at home while I was attending an all-girls school with pregnant teenagers. I had to take care of her kids and make dinner for everyone on a daily basis. Again, I found myself being taken advantage of, and during a time when I really needed someone to take care of me.

For months, Gloria abused and mistreated me to the point where I was reliving the brothel days with her mother all over again. She even got me a fake ID card and made me work in a bar where I was also the subject of abuse by men who frequented the place.

I lived with Gloria until I had my baby, and when my daughter was three months old, we ran away. We walked the streets and often found places to sleep. One night, I was standing outside a night club looking for food, and a guy approached me. He felt very bad for us and offered to let us stay with him. I don't know how I trusted him, but desperation kicked in and I had to take a chance. The guy lived in a small storage room near the club. He had managed to make a home out of it. It was clean and organized and much better than the streets. It was not big enough to fit all three of us, but we managed.

Julio was extremely nice to us. He provided food for me, and formula for my daughter. He even found me a babysitter so that I could continue to go to school. He worked in a local restaurant and used to send most of his money to his parents in Mexico. This made me respect him even more. I could not have met a better person with whom to stay.

One day, Gloria managed to find out where I lived and called the police. I was only sixteen then. The police came to our place and took me and my daughter to a group home for girls. I was glad Julio wasn't there because they would have probably arrested him.

I could not speak English well at that time, but I was assigned a lawyer who spoke Spanish. He advised me to stay in the home until I was eighteen because he was fighting to get legal residence and medical benefits for me and my baby.

When I turned nineteen, I was finally awarded legal status. With the help of my lawyer and social worker, I was able to qualify for **transitional** housing where I stayed for a few years.

In 2013, I decided to take ESL classes in an adult school, which was more like a learning center. I completed the ESL program, then took GED courses and studied until I received a high school diploma in 2014. That opened up the door for me to attend a local community College.

In 2017, I completed my AA degree in Behaviorial and Natural Science. I am currently enrolled in the Respiratory Therapy Program at the same college and working as a care giver in an assisted living facility where I take care of the elderly.

Right now, I have my own place, and have taken in a friend who is currently going through a divorce. We support each other and attend the same program. My goal is to graduate and get a job in a hospital to help the elderly who have breathing problems. I also want to be a role model for my daughter and show her that with hard work and determination, we can overcome obstacles and succeed in life.

My journey has been **undoubtedly** very difficult, but it is gradually getting easier and simpler and I envision a better and brighter future for me and my daughter. I feel proud that I have come a long way and can actually help others in difficult situations.

I. Writing Questions:

After reading this chapter, please go back to your annotations and write **three** WH-questions (questions that begin with what, when, where, who, which, how, how many, etc.), and **three** Yes/no questions (questions that begin with is, are, was, were, do, does, did, etc.).

WH-Questions:

1.

2.

3.

Yes/No Questions:

1.

2.

3.

Thinking about Problems and Solutions: Having read Evie's story and what she has been through, imagine that you were a victim of a similar circumstance. What would you have done differently to get out of your bad situation?

II. VOCABULARY WORDS: Below, write the definition for each word, either by using context clues, or by looking them up in the dictionary.

1. pimp	13. miraculously	24. hostile
2. brothel	14. storm out	25. nauseous
3. bribe	15. barn	26. furious
4. mistreat	16. survive	27. refuse
5. abuse	17. merchandize	28. unbearable
6. disgustingly	18. axe	29. reject
7. revolting	19. suffocate	30. transitional
8. shelter	20. judgmental	31. undoubtedly
9. derailed	21. confusingly	
10. vultures	22. stump	
11. prey	23. pre-determined	
12. coyotes		

III. Use five new words from the table above to write an original sentence for each word.

1.

2.

3.

4.

5.

IV. PARTS OF SPEECH: There are eight parts of speech in the English language, and they are the following: noun, pronoun, verb, adverb, adjective, preposition, conjunction and interjection. These parts of speech tell us how words function grammatically and in terms of meaning within a sentence.

At this point, we will only focus on the following four parts of speech:

1. Noun
Nouns are names of people, places, things, or ideas. Nouns are often used with articles (a, an, the), but not all the time.

woman ... East Los Angeles College... table... success
Example: **A woman** worked very hard in her job in order to gain **success.**

2. Verb
Verbs express actions or states of being. Verbs must agree with their subjects in number. They can also express different tenses (present, past, etc.).

run... are... read... appear
Example: He **ran** to his children who **were** in front of the school.

3. Adverb
Adverbs modify or describe verbs, adjectives, or other adverbs. They never describe a noun. They often end in -ly.

softly... extremely... usually... well
Example: The tall man was wearing an **unusually** large hat, but he **quickly** took it off when he saw me.

4. Adjective
Adjectives modify or describe nouns or pronouns. They usually answer the question of which one, how many, and what kind.

Amazing... old... red... intelligent
Example: I usually go to many **great** concerts, but this concert was **amazing**, and I am very **happy** that I came with you.

V. In the table below, identify the part of speech for each word.

Word	Part of Speech (noun, verb, adjective, or adverb)
1. brothel	( )
2. disgusting	( )
3. shelter	( )
4. vulture	( )
5. confusingly	( )
6. merchandize	( )
7. prey	( )
8. suffocate	( )
9. undoubtedly	( )
10. stump	( )

VI. Internet Search: Do research on transitional housing or group homes for women. Write down any new or important information that you learn about these places and share them with the class.

Aracely from Santa Rosa, El Salvador: Just My Luck

Part I

Thinking back to when I decided to leave my country and come to the United States still breaks my heart and makes me teary-eyed. I used to hear the expression, **"grass is greener on the other side"** and always wondered if there was a piece of that beautiful green grass out there for me.

I lived in a small town called, Santa Rosa, which is a village within a tiny district in El Salvador where people mostly did farm work. The crops of choice were beans and corn, and some people also raised cattle, which provided another source of income.

Our town lost many of its residents in the 1970's and 80's during the El Salvador civil war. The majority of them emigrated to the United States to places where the cost of living was affordable and jobs in construction and farming were available. So, the town suffered greatly for decades until recently when roads were paved, and cars and busses were able to access it.

I stayed with my mother and siblings along with my two children, as I had been separated from my husband for a few years.

We lived in a small house that my mother had inherited from my grandparents. My mother did not have any farm land, so she worked in a local factory that manufactured plastic topper ware. As for me, I was doing some clerical work here and there in addition to some odd jobs that I could find in town. Most of the time, I was taking care of my children and four siblings when my mother was at work.

One day when my older brother, Carlos opened the refrigerator and found it **practically** empty, he started yelling at me.

"You and your kids eat everything, and there's nothing left for us."

I did not know what to say. I had never thought about it in that way before. My legs were shaking, and I felt **dizzy**. I stood idle for a long time just trying to process what I had just heard. It was then when a million ideas came to my head, and all of them involved leaving that house, that environment, that **poisonous** life with no hope in sight.

That day, I cried on and off till my mother came home from work. By then, my eyes were **puffy,** and I barely had any energy to stand up. I didn't eat or drink anything. Actually, there wasn't much to eat or drink anyway, other than water and old molded **tortillas**. Even if we had food, I was too upset to eat.

My children and siblings had asked me earlier if I was going to cook something, but I didn't have any money to buy groceries and was hoping my mother would bring us something on her way home.

"Aracely! Aracely! Come help me carry these bags into the house." My mom yelled from outside the house.

I was very happy to see bags of groceries in her hands. My poor mother had carried the bags all the way from the bus stop, four blocks away. She had worked eight hours and took two busses afterward to get home.

Nothing in our household seemed to be OK. The only thing that was **consoling** me was that soon, the kids would all go back to school, and I could get some kind of a job to be able to contribute something to the household.

I **constantly** thought about what my brother said to me, and that weight heavily on shoulders. I started to watch what I ate because I did not want him to think I ate more than I needed or deserved. I also told my kids not to open the fridge unless they asked me first. It was a horrible feeling on a daily basis, but I had to swallow my pride and bear the situation.

"Sit down Mama. Sit down." I will put everything away. I took her by the hand and **lightly** placed her on the sofa. I almost fell.

"Aracely, how was everything today?" Mom asked.

I don't think that she had seen my face yet.

"Things were OK, Mama. Let me cook some dinner for everyone. You just rest."

"Get one of your sisters to help you!" Mama demanded.

My sisters were very lazy and always waited for me or my mom to do everything for them, and my kids were only six and eight. Of course, we wouldn't dare ask my brother, Carlos to help in the kitchen. That would be unheard of, since he was the oldest male in the house.

I didn't understand that double standard because he didn't even have a job, nor did he have anything else to offer or contribute to the family. Nevertheless, it was understood that nobody was to bother him.

During the next few months, we were barely getting by, and Christmas was soon **approaching**. My mother started stressing out about the holidays and how we weren't going to **afford** buying anything new.

In the meantime, many ideas were still **rattling** my brain, and I wanted to ask my mother if it was at all possible for me to try to go to California, as many people at that time were doing, to work and send them money. I just didn't know how to sell her the idea of leaving my children behind.

I knew that crossing the border would be a very difficult and **arduous** journey for adults, let alone children. We had heard about many stories of people even dying before they were able to cross. Still, I wanted to take that risk.

The situation at home wasn't **bearable** anymore, for any of us. Something needed to change. Nobody else in the family seemed to have any drive or interest to take the leap. There is only so much a human can **endure**, and our family was on the verge of **collapsing**. I knew it had to be me.

After what my family and I had been through, I was ready to undertake anything. So, I got up the courage and sat with my mother to discuss the possibility. I knew that she would have to leave her job to take care of my children if I were able to leave.

"Mommy, I was thinking that maybe Sandra can start working now. She is already twenty years old, and Carlos is thirty and is still living here and not doing anything to help us. What do you think?" I blurted it all out very quickly because my heart was racing.

"I do not want Sandra to work. It's too dangerous for a pretty girl like her." Mom **justified**, and as if to say that I was not as pretty, and it was OK for me to work and be in danger.

"Carlos has been looking for a job for a long time, but there are no jobs available, honey." She added.

"I think there are jobs, but he won't accept any. He is just waiting around for things to happen. He needs to be out there looking for a job every day until he finds one." I protested.

"Leave Carlos to me, mija (my daughter in Spanish)." She insisted. Mom always protected Carlos.

"And what about Sandra? Being pretty won't get her anywhere in life. She needs to have work experience and see the world from a different **perspective** rather than sitting here watching **soap operas** all day long. Why do you think she's still a little girl? She's twenty years old. She doesn't want to go to college or work. She's just waiting for a man to marry her and take care of her." I was beginning to get angry and frustrated. Mama seemed to have different standards for each of us.

"Wait a minute! What is going on with you today? Why are you all of a sudden concerned with your brother and sister and whether they work or not? I take care of them. You don't need to worry." Mom calmly told me.

"Well, Mommy. I need to ask you something." I started to soften my voice a bit.

"Yes? What is it?"

"I was thinking that if Carlos and Sandra could get jobs, then you don't have to work anymore. Maybe you can stay home, and I can, maybe, go to California and work. I will work and send you all money." I nervously and carefully suggested.

"No. No. No. It's too dangerous for you and your children. I won't let you go."

"Well, I was thinking to leave my kids with you until I find a job. Then I can try to bring them to live with me. Maybe I'll be able to bring all of you to California one day. Wouldn't that be nice, Mommy?"

"Ahhhhh! Now I understand why you want me to quit my job. No. That won't happen." My mom was completely against the idea.

I. Writing Questions:

After reading this chapter, please go back to your annotations and write **three** WH-questions (questions that begin with what, when, where, who, which, how, how many, etc.), and **three** Yes/no questions (questions that begin with is, are, was, were, do, does, did, etc.).

WH-Questions:

1.

2.

3.

Yes/No Questions:

1.

2.

3.

Critical Thinking: It is obvious that Aracely's mother treats each of her children differently and her expectations of them varies across age, and gender. What is your analysis of why she does that? Provide examples from the story to support your analysis.

II. VOCABULARY WORDS: Below, write the definition for each word, either by using context clues, or by looking them up in the dictionary.

1. Practically	9. approach	17. justify
2. dizzy	10. afford	18. perspective
3. poisonous	11. rattle	19. soap opera
4. puffy	12. arduous	
5. tortilla	13. bearable	
6. console	14. drive	
7. constantly	15. endure	
8. lightly	16. collapse	

III. Use five new words from the table above to write an original sentence for each word.

1.

2.

3.

4.

5.

Aracely from Santa Rosa, El Salvador: Just My Luck

Part II

That night, I thought that the only way I could do this was to put my mother on the spot and just leave. This way, she would have to just accept it.

I thought of leaving her and my children a note explaining why I was doing it. I know it was selfish of me to even think that way, but I had the best

intentions in my mind and in my heart. After all, the opportunities were not exactly knocking on my door.

One day before Christmas, I left the house very early in the morning. I had been saving money for my journey. I knew I would have to **bribe** some people along the way in order to get to my **destination**.

I walked a few blocks and took the bus from our town, Santa Rosa, in the city of San Juan to the Guatemalan border. I spent the night in a cheap motel until the morning.

I asked around to see how I could cross the Guatemala/Mexico border. I followed the directions that an old man had given me and walked until sunset.

I ended up near a river where a group of people with some children were waiting to cross. Every time I looked at the small children, I was thankful that I did not have mine with me. They were cold and hungry and seemed very **confused**. They kept asking their parents, "where are we going? Are we almost there?"

I followed the group, and we all stepped into the freezing water together. I only had my backpack with me. The men took off all their clothes except for the underwear, but the women kept their clothes on. We all held our backpacks above our heads as to keep our belongings dry.

As we walked further, I had this burning pain in my feet, which soon turned to complete **numbness**. My soaked clothes made the rest of my body shiver, as if the trip wasn't hard enough already. I don't even remember how my body was moving. All I knew at that time was that I had to do what I needed to do in order to get to the other side.

Once we crossed the river and stepped onto land, I realized we were in the Mexican state of Vera Cruz. I knew I had a cousin there who operated a truck station. I just didn't know the address. I kept looking in phone books and asking around until I found his business number. I gave the number to the group leader, and he promised to call me when they we were ready to get on the next train.

When I called my cousin, he said he would pick me up from a gas station close to where I was. I was lucky because he was only forty minutes away. On the way to his house, he told me that I could stay with his family until I received word from the leader of our group that I had a seat on the next train.

Five days later, I received news to meet the group leader by a specific train station. My cousin drove me in his big truck across the state of Vera Cruz. I boarded the train and got in my assigned seat. We rode to the city of Coatzacoalcos, and from there to Tierra Blanca, to San Rafael and then to Poza Rica where I took a bus to Nuevo Laredo.

When we arrived, it was all white. As far as the eye could see, the area was covered in snow. I had never in my life seen anything like this up close. Although I was extremely cold, and my feet were numb, somehow, I felt peaceful and tried to enjoy the moment of experiencing something new and beautiful.

"Do not say anything to each other and just get on the train." A couple of men told all of us.

I don't remember much about the ride or how long it took because I was in and out of sleep the whole way. I do remember that I did not want to talk to anyone on the train as not to get in trouble, and my stomach was **growling**.

A man next to me whispered in my ear, "The water in the Rio Grande is probably freezing now, and it is **going to be Hell** to cross."

I did not respond. The time between getting off the train and crossing the river is a **blur**.

I woke up and found myself under a bridge. I was shivering and **soaking** wet. I sat there for a few minutes trying to recall what had happened on the trip. I felt **disoriented** and confused.

Where am I? How did I get here? What am I doing?

As I slowly tried to **regain** my **composure**, I realized that I had crossed the Rio Grande (this river divides Mexico and the U.S.A. at the Mexico-Texas border). I do not remember crossing the water with a group of people, though.

Did I just cross the Rio Grande by myself? I could not recall anything from that part of the journey. I was weak and felt like I had lost my **coordination** when I tried to stand up.

A man walked by and stared at me for a while. Then he offered to give me a small blanket. He just handed it to me and disappeared. As I came out from underneath the bridge, I read a big sign. It said, "San Antonio Bridge, Texas." I started walking to see where I needed to go next. I came face-to-face with a Native American man.

"Where are you going?" He asked.

At first, I was scared and hesitated to answer. But then, he said that I looked cold and seemed like I needed help. He had probably seen many people like me going through that area.

"I can take you where you need to go. Did you cross the border?"

"Yes. I need to go to Houston to look for work." I told him the short version of my story. He handed me a bologna sandwich. It was my first time eating that kind of food. I **devoured** it in a few seconds. I was **starving**.

We drove to Houston, and I told him the rest of my sad story on the way. Every time I mentioned my children, my throat would tighten, and I wasn't able to breathe. The man was very understanding and listened to me patiently, offering me some consoling words every now and then. For the most part, I was the one doing the talking. Thank goodness he spoke Spanish.

In Houston, the man took me to this house where "this nice family helps people like you," he said. When we arrived, I met a lady named Rosa, who helped me get a room in her house. She gave me some clothes, a towel and a bar of soap and showed me where to take a bath. It had been days since I took a shower or sat in a bathtub with hot water.

"You can stay here for two months." Rosa told me at dinner. I sat with her and six other people who seemed to be in a similar situation to mine. Rosa fed me, clothed me, and listened to my story every day, as she did for the other six people. She was also trying to find work for all of us, but to no avail.

I did not want to be a burden on Rosa anymore, and seven people were a lot for her and her family to help. One morning after I had been there for a couple of weeks, I told her that I had a childhood friend whom I had not seen in years, and that she lived in California.

"Even though I greatly appreciate your **hospitality**, and everything you have done for me, I would like to go to Los Angeles and find a job. Maybe my old friend could help me. I need to start sending my family money as I promised I would." I cried. "Rosa, could you please help me find my friend? I begged.

When we finally found her number, I called Maria. I told her my story. She said that she would send me an airplane ticket to come to Los Angeles.

"We will figure something out when you get here, my dear friend." She told me.

One thing I had always wanted to have was an education. When my mother was very poor, I had to drop out from school because I had to work to help her. But I remember that in the building where I once lived with my children, the social worker told me that there was a program in which a student would live with me for a month to **observe** the type of life that

I lived and how I educated my children as well as what kind of food we ate or bought. The student would do a case study and share the **findings** with his or her university program.

I had accepted the offer, and the student came to my house three days later. He spent the next three weeks with us. He documented many things and took photos and videos of me and my family. I was promised a payment of $500.00 in return, which was going to help us **tremendously**.

The student's presence there was often **inconvenient** and **awkward**, but we got through it alright. Besides, part of the deal was that the student was given a stipend to buy food for himself and for us. It was a win-win situation at that time, I guess.

Afterwards, the organizers of the program invited me to the University to attend the student's presentation and to also ask me questions. In addition, as part of the program, I was supposed to go through a special training on how to be an **effective** and positive parent.

I was happy to attend the training because they offered breakfast and lunch, and I could bring my children with me. Also, I was hoping I would learn something new.

This was when my interest to be back in school was **reborn**. Before that, I had felt scared whenever I thought about the idea of going to college one day because my mother used to say, "Universities are only for the rich people, not for us my dear daughter."

I. Writing Questions:

After reading this chapter, please go back to your annotations and write **three** WH-questions (questions that begin with what, when, where, who, which, how, how many, etc.), and **three** Yes/no questions (questions that begin with is, are, was, were, do, does, did, etc.).

WH-Questions:

1.

2.

3.

Yes/No Questions:

1.

2.

3.

Discussion Question: What is Aracely's mother's view on education regarding her own children? Provide examples to support your answers.

II. VOCABULARY WORDS: Below, write the definition for each word, either by using context clues, or by looking them up in the dictionary.

1. intentions	10. regain	18. findings
2. bribe	11. composure	19. tremendously
3. destination	12. coordination	20. inconvenient
4. confused	13. short version	21. awkward
5. numbness	14. devour	22. effective
6. growl	15. starve	23. reborn
7. blur	16. hospitality	
8. soak	17. observe	
9. disoriented		

III. Use five new words from the table above to write an original sentence for each word.

1.

2.

3.

4.

5.

Aracely from Santa Rosa, El Salvador: Just My Luck

Part III

When I came to the United States, I did not know I was **pregnant**. I had been dating a man back in Santa Rosa, but nothing was serious about our relationship. When I found out about the pregnancy, the first thing that came to my mind was to have an **abortion**. I had no clue what I was doing at that time, and to add a child to the **equation** was going to make my life a hundred times more difficult.

Somehow, my friend convinced me to go ahead with the pregnancy. She said that the government would help me financially to take care of the baby's needs and all the medical expenses.

"Besides, you do not want to get rid of the baby, Aracely." She said. "We are Catholic, remember?" She tried to me feel **guilty**.

The bottom line was that I decided to keep the baby but had to find a job right away. My friend told me about a job not too far away from where she was living. I remember I had to go in for an interview and I did not speak much English, but the lady of the house said that she wanted her children to learn Spanish.

So, I was supposed to be a cheap nanny and a skilled language teacher at the same time. Although I ended up doing everything else in that house for $ 10.00 per day, I was still satisfied because I did not have legal documents to be **picky** about the job or the pay.

Two weeks into the job, the husband started making unwanted sexual advances toward me. I kept **rejecting** him every day and even told him that I would leave if he continued **harassing** me. He did not care.

He tried to push me into the laundry room one day while I was pregnant. I fought him off and started screaming. When he heard his wife open the front door, he stopped.

I never said anything about it to the wife. I think the husband was afraid I would say something one day. So, he paid me for the week and demanded that I did not return the following day.

"If my wife called you, you will say that you found another job. Do you understand?" He looked at me with bulgy eyes and shook my shoulder back and forth.

I gathered my things at the end of the day and stayed with my friend. She told me that I could stay with her until I gave birth to my daughter. Then I started looking for a job again.

Another friend, whom I had made while in Los Angeles, told me about a young woman who offered me $ 80.00 per week just to take care of the house and feed the dog. The deal also included a room for me and my daughter. It was a great set up where the lady said that I could also work somewhere else during the day when I was done with my work. This way I could make more money.

Unfortunately, this never happened because my baby cried a lot, and I could barely finish my work at the lady's house.

During the first year, it was extremely hard for me to work. I had no idea what cleaning materials I had to use for different things. There was some glass cleaner, wood cleaner, tile cleaner, toilet cleaner, leather polish, shower and bathtub cleaner and many other chemicals that I had to learn about when doing the laundry. It was not that **complicated** where I came from. We had one form of household cleaner for everything.

The lady of the house brought a former housekeeper to teach me all about house **chores** and what to use for each part of the house. Sometimes I forgot and used the wrong thing, but I did not say anything. Day by day, I learned to be a good housekeeper.

Because my daughter used to cry a lot, and I did not have anyone to help me take care of her, I left the nanny job and started selling **cosmetics** by going door-to-door in my neighborhood just to make enough money to support myself and the baby. I also send money to my mother and siblings, as I had promised.

I was living in my friend's house where we were thirteen people in a one-bedroom apartment. After fifteen months, I saw that the situation had gone from bad to worse. I needed to get out at any cost.

One day, I met a man through a **mutual** friend. We dated for a short time, but we quickly decided to move in together and get married.

Oscar, that was his name, gradually became more controlling and jealous. I had to keep quiet and just take it because my daughter and I had nowhere else to go.

A few months into the marriage, I got pregnant with my fourth child, and at that point, I was only able to send enough money for meals to my children in El Salvador. It seemed like things were never going to get better for me or my family back home.

When my son was born, I was seriously thinking about divorcing Oscar and returning to live with my mother and my other two children. The **tragedy** was that my mother had died before I could make the trip. I was not able to go to her funeral.

My brother, Carlos was furious with me. He said he had to borrow money from all the neighbors to pay for the funeral and burial cost. This truly broke my heart.

I felt very guilty, and the burden weighed very heavily on my shoulders. *Who will take care of my two children? Who will take care of my siblings?* There was only one thing I could do to rectify any chance of reunifying with my children and helping my brothers and sisters.

The father of my first two kids, Daniel, had a business visa and traveled often between the U.S.A. and El Salvador. Even though I did not want to associate myself with him in any way, I still had to go to him for help. I asked him if he could arrange for a way to bring the children to me. At first, he **hesitated**, especially after he found out that I was remarried and had two more children. But when I told him that my mother had passed away, and nobody was able to take care of them, he found a way to finally bring them to me.

For a while, my new husband and my kids were not getting along at all, but when my oldest daughter was able to work after school at a local restaurant, and my son started helping me a little around the house, things improved, but my husband still had some anger and jealousy issues.

Whenever we had guests over, my husband would watch my every move, and later question me about **silly** and **trivial** things. I dealt with him in the best way that I could to keep our family together, but sometimes I thought I could not take it anymore.

One day, when I thought things were slowly getting better, and our lives had become a bit more peaceful, I received a letter in the mail from the Department of Motor Vehicles (DMV). It stated that my driver's license was suspended.

Upon further **investigation**, my husband found out that the family I had worked for as a nanny had a car accident, and the wife simply gave my name to the police officer. She had claimed that she had her driver's license at home at the time of the accident.

This took a few months to **resolve**, and the lady had to serve some jail time and pay a penalty, but my life became so much more complicated as I could not drive myself or the kids anywhere with a suspended license.

At that time, my husband's behavior became a lot worse toward me and my two older kids. It was as if he was trying very hard to make our lives as difficult as possible so that we would leave. It seemed like we could not do anything right. Anything triggered his anger.

Fearing for the safety and **sanity** of all of us, I started to secretly hide away whatever money I could save from my food **allowance** and my daughter's job. I had been planning to leave and divorce my husband after we all received legal status.

When we finally had enough money for an apartment, I told the kids. It was as if they had won the lottery.

It has been thirty-one years since I moved to the U.S.A., and life is still difficult here, but I started going to college a few years ago, and my English language skills have improved greatly. So, I have been able to work in many different places to provide for my family. My four kids have gone to college, and two have already graduated. My other two children are still trying to find their way in this world, which is Ok with me.

I guess if you ask me now after all these years if my journey to the U.S.A. was worth it, I would say, not in this way, but for immigrants like me, we often don't have many choices. I guess if I had to compare my current situation to when I was living in El Salvador, I would then say it has been worth it.

I. Writing Questions:

After reading this chapter, please go back to your annotations and write **three** WH-questions (questions that begin with what, when, where, who, which, how, how many, etc.), and **three** Yes/no questions (questions that begin with is, are, was, were, do, does, did, etc.).

WH-Questions:

1.

2.

3.

Yes/No Questions:

1.

2.

3.

Discussion Question: In one of her many jobs, Aracely takes on a position of a nanny, but soon endures sexual advances made by the man of the house. She is afraid to say anything to his wife because she fears the idea losing her job. Do you think Aracely would have kept quiet if she was documented? How could she have handled the situation differently? Provide at least two scenarios.

II. VOCABULARY WORDS: Below, write the definition for each word, either by using context clues, or by looking them up in the dictionary.

1. pregnant	8. complicated	15. trivial
2. abortion	9. chores	16. investigation
3. equation	10. cosmetics	17. resolve
4. guilty	11. mutual	18. Fear
5. picky	12. tragedy	19. sanity
6. reject	13. hesitate	20. allowance
7. harass	14. silly	

III. Use five new words from the table above to write an original sentence for each word.

1.

2.

3.

4.

5.

IV. Internet Search: Do a search on the Rio Grande (the Big River) and immigrants and their children who have crossed or attempted to cross it to get to the USA side of the border. Then, write a short paragraph using your own words to explain to your classmates what you learned.

V. In the table below, identify the part of speech for each word.

Word	Part of Speech (noun, verb, adjective, or adverb)
1. tragedy	( )
2. sanity	( )
3. hesitate	( )
4. allowance	( )
5. reject	( )
6. guilty	( )
7. equation	( )
8. abortion	( )
9. trivial	( )
10. complicated	( )
11. tremendously	( )
12. disoriented	( )
13. composure	( )
14. intention	( )

Mei Lin from Tsinan, China:
The Hidden Baby

They call my city, "The Jewel between Beijing and Shanghai." It's also often called, "The City of Springs," as it has hundreds of them. The famous actor, Jackie Chan and I come from that big city and it is called, Tsinan, which is located in central China and is the capital of Shandong province.

I was born and raised in Tsinan, and in my family, there were my parents, an older brother and me. My father was an accountant, and my mother was a homemaker. I was very lucky to have grown up in a **household** where we were **financially** able to have all life's **conveniences,** and my brother and I could go to good schools, unlike many people in our city.

After I graduated from high school, I majored in nursing, something that I had always thought of doing, because I loved helping people. I must say that I did not struggle much in any area of my life because my parents made it very easy for me to excel and finish school. All I had to do was study, sleep and eat. I was never one who liked to go out or party, so I never got myself in any trouble with my parents. I just focused all my energy on my school and made sure I received the highest grades possible.

When I was finished with the nursing program, I was able to get a job at a university hospital as an RN (Registered Nurse). At the age of twenty-three, I got married and one year later, my husband and I had a son. All the pieces were falling in the right places for me and my family, and we were very grateful for everything we had.

In the years that followed, I became pregnant several times and had to **abort** the pregnancy because of the one-child per family policy in China. There were **severe consequences** if couples had a second or third child. The **authorities brutally enforced** the law with **harsh punishments**. If women were caught, they were taken by the police to a clinic where they would be given a shot in the arm and then either forced to get an abortion or be **sterilized** against their will. In addition, the women would have to pay huge fines, which placed a great burden on their families.

You might be asking why I wasn't careful, but as it was, my body was not responding to many forms of protection. Therefore, every time it happened, I was forced to get an **abortion**, which broke my heart every single time and left me depressed for months after. All in all, I had six abortions within ten years.

Finally, in 2012, after having worked in the same hospital for eighteen years, I **confided** in our head nurse that I was pregnant, and that my intention was to keep the baby. My husband and I felt very strongly that we wanted another baby. We were able to financially make it without worrying, and I wasn't getting any younger.

I had shared with the head nurse that I would come to the USA and have the baby, then go back to China and resume my position at work. I asked her nicely not to say anything to anyone in the hospital as to not get me in trouble with the authorities.

I gathered all the necessary papers and was able to get a visitor's visa and bring my ten-year-old son with me. I was six months pregnant at that time. My husband stayed behind because he had to continue working to support us. It was very difficult, as I didn't have anyone in the USA to help me. We stayed in a hotel in Alhambra, California for a week while I searched on the Internet for a place to rent.

Once we settled down, I started asking around (Chinese people whom I encountered anywhere) about how to get to a medical center and see a doctor for free. Some nice lady who was sitting on a bench at a bus stop directed me to a free walk-in clinic nearby. When she saw that I was not knowledgeable about the area, she took the time to teach me how to read the bus schedule and take the right bus to the clinic.

"Good morning! How can we help you?" A young woman at the front desk of the clinic greeted us in Chinese.

Right away, I felt safe. I saw a doctor who was also Chinese. He asked me many questions and took the time to record my answers on a notepad. He then ordered blood work and an Ultrasound test to make sure the baby was growing normally.

I visited the clinic often and actually thought of the doctor and the people there as my second family away from home. They were the closest people I had in the U.S. **Frequenting** the clinic and places around the area, I was able to learn many things about the free resources available for people in my position.

As I got closer to giving birth, my energy level decreased dramatically. I could not leave the house as often, which made it hard for my son because he loved going to the park to play with some friends he had made in the neighborhood.

Life seemed very difficult, and at times, I felt lonely and helpless. On top of not being able to go out and do activities with my son, I could not contribute financially to our family. My husband had to work twice as hard to send us money each month to pay for all our expenses. I had to pay for rent and utilities, purchase a car to get around and take my son to school, pay for food and all other necessities.

The financial **burden** was beginning to weigh heavily on our family, and I was in no position to work. Who was going to hire a pregnant woman who didn't speak English and had another child for whom she had to care? Even if I worked somewhere, who would take care of my son? Who would take him to and pick him up from school?

The day to have my baby quickly came, and I had to go to the closest hospital, which was five miles away. Another Chinese lady I had met told me that I should simply call 911 when "the time comes," and they would come quickly and take me to the hospital. So, I did just that. I called 911. The person who answered was asking me a lot of questions. I could not understand much. I just kept saying, "Baby! Baby!"

After trying to get information from me for a couple of minutes, the lady on the phone asked me if I spoke Vietnamese or Chinese.

"Chinese, Chinese." I screamed loudly. I was having contractions and was in a lot of pain. My son was sitting down watching cartoons.

"OK, Ma'am. I will get someone to **translate** for you." At least that is what I thought she was going to do.

Sure enough, a Chinese woman spoke to me, and I was able to give her my address and tell her that I was having the baby and needed help. Ten minutes later, the **ambulance** came to my place. The **paramedics** did not know what to do with my son. They realized I did not have anyone in the house to stay with him. So, he had to sit next to me in the back of the ambulance. I knew it was going to be very **traumatic** for him, but I had no other choice. He kept looking at me with teary eyes.

"You are OK, Mom. You are OK." He kept telling me in Chinese. Then he would ask the paramedics, "Is my mom going to be OK?"

After I gave birth to our baby girl, I was getting ready to leave the U.S.A. and reunite with my husband, but when I contacted the head nurse to tell her the news, she advised me strongly not to go back to work because I no longer had the job.

Apparently, she had shared my secret with a co-worker, and then the news spread all over the hospital.

Soon after that, fifteen people wrote letters to the hospital president to tell him that I had had another child. They also told him that I was already pregnant when I was working and had kept it a secret for six months.

This was a huge problem because not only had I lied to my superiors, which would carry some legal consequences, but I would have no job when I went back. No hospital would hire me after that because I would need a recommendation letter from my current employer.

Basically, my career was over in China.

Since we weren't presented with many options, my husband suggested that we apply for **Political Asylum** status in the U.S.A. This was going to take time, and as of then, my husband had not seen our baby girl yet. She was now twenty-two months. I wasn't able to go back to China for fear of possible punishment, and my husband wasn't able to leave his job because that was our only source of income.

Feeling **helpless** and **hopeless**, I recently decided to go to a local community college and take English courses in order to look for a job later. First, I needed to work to stay busy, and second, I needed to help pay for the extra expenses now that I am paying a babysitter to stay with my daughter while I am in school.

So far, school is going well, and I have met many nice teachers and students. Slowly, my kids and I are adapting to living here, separated from my husband, but we are hoping that he will be able to come and visit us for two weeks next year.

This experience has truly taught me to be completely **independent** in a strange place and to also be patient. It hasn't been easy for any of us, and I spend many nights crying about how I lost my job in the hospital in China. I cry about all the abortions that the Chinese government imposed on me. I cry about how I ended up alone without any family support. Nevertheless, I tell myself that the situation is temporary, and I hope that soon things will change for us.

On the other hand, going to school has helped me **tremendously** to stay focused, and every time I complete a semester, I feel accomplished and have a little bit more **confidence** in myself to continue living and taking care of my children. I cannot wait till next year when my husband comes to visit us and meet our daughter, Sophie for the first time.

I. Writing Questions:

After reading this chapter, please go back to your annotations and write **three** WH-questions (questions that begin with what, when, where, who, which, how, how many, etc.), and **three** Yes/no questions (questions that begin with is, are, was, were, do, does, did, etc.).

WH-Questions:

1.

2.

3.

Yes/No Questions:

1.

2.

3.

Discussion Question: Mei Lin makes the mistake of telling the head nurse at her work about her secret. What was the outcome of that mistake? Provide evidence to support your answers.

II. VOCABULARY WORDS: Below, write the definition for each word, either by using context clues, or by looking them up in the dictionary.

15. household	25. punishment	35. political asylum
16. financially	26. sterilize	36. helpless
17. convenience	27. confide	37. hopeless
18. abort	28. frequent	38. independent
19. severe	29. burden	39. tremendously
20. consequence	30. translate	40. confidence
21. authorities	31. ambulance	
22. brutally	32. paramedic	
23. enforce	33. traumatic	
24. harsh	34. apparently	

III. Use five new words from the table above to write an original sentence for each word.

1.

2.

3.

4.

5.

IV. In the table below, identify the part of speech for each word.

Word	Part of Speech (noun, verb, adjective, or adverb)
1. household	( )
2. financially	( )
3. convenience	( )
4. confide	( )
5. severe	( )
6. traumatic	( )
7. apparently	( )
8. independent	( )
9. helpless	( )
10. burden	( )

V. Internet Search: Do research on the one-child policy in China. Then, write a short paragraph using your own words to explain to your classmates what you learned on the topic when the policy was in effect and what changes have occurred in the recent years.

Juliana from Beltrán, Mexico:
Bad Decisions

Part I

"Juliana, go make dinner for your brothers!" My mom would yell out almost every evening. She would come home very tired from being on her feet all day. She and my father would usually have something to eat before they took two or three buses to get home. Both of my parents worked in factories, and I was the oldest child who had most of the **responsibilities** around the house.

I was born in a very small village called, Beltrán in Mexico and grew up with four siblings in Estación Rojo, an **adjacent** village. I spent most of my childhood and young adulthood there until I was eighteen and had graduated from high school. I was always **anxious** to leave home and the difficult daily life we had.

When I used to hear stories of **adventure** from college students in town, I could not wait to get to a university and finally have some fun and freedom. I didn't want to hear things like, "Juliana, make dinner! Juliana, help your brother Jesus with his homework! Juliana, see what your sister Maria wants! Juliana, go bathe your brothers, go clean the house, go make breakfast, go to the store and get some **groceries**," and so on and so on.

My friends, Consuelo and Lolita were sitting on an old bench outside our house one day. We were talking about **random** things, like boys, school, fashion and other things that I do not remember. We had all been waiting for news from the university to see whether we were going to be accepted. So, we were also waiting for the mail carrier to deliver our mail. Even though I was excited about opening the letter, all three of us had decided to wait until we all received our letters and planned to open them together.

George, the mail carrier, approached as he **stretched** his arm toward me. He handed me a stack of envelopes. I sifted through the stack slowly and carefully until I saw a letter from the university.

"I have to run home and check the mail." Consuelo got up and **dashed** home.

"Me too!" Lolita excitedly said.

Three days later, all three of us had received our letters from La Universidad Autónoma De Sinaloa (Freelance University, Sinaloa). We were arguing about who was going to open her letter first, but finally decided that we would do it at the same time. I watched Consuelo's eyebrows rise. Then,

Lolita's **jaw** dropped open, and she screamed in excitement. I still hadn't even looked at my own letter.

"I'm in! I'm in!" Consuelo sang and danced around the living room.

"Me too! Me too!" Lolita shouted.

I was a bit nervous to read my letter, but I looked up, and both of my friends were waiting to hear from me. I slowly unfolded the paper and **peeked** in to prepare myself **mentally** before I gave them a reaction. As soon as I read the word, "Congratulations," I was relieved. I screamed. I yelled. I jumped up and down.

That night, we spent hours drinking **Tequila** and talking at a local bar. The following day, we were just trying to **recover** from our hangovers.

For three months, my **amigas** (friends) and I were preparing to move away. My father had found us a small apartment, which wasn't very far from the university. We shared the rent and all expenses and times we had some fun, but things did not run **smoothly** for long.

We started arguing over trivial things, like who was going to wash the dishes and who was responsible for buying food and other items for the house. We even argued about the sleeping arrangements and who was allowed to come over or spend the night at our place. Living together was not fun or comfortable anymore.

This is when I decided to get my own place. It meant that I had to get a job if I didn't want my parents to be **burdened**, especially because money was already running low back at home, and my parents couldn't help me much financially.

I. Writing Questions:

After reading this chapter, please go back to your annotations and write **three** WH-questions (questions that begin with what, when, where, who, which, how, how many, etc.), and **three** Yes/no questions (questions that begin with is, are, was, were, do, does, did, etc.).

WH-Questions:

1.

2.

3.

Yes/No Questions:

1.

2.

3.

- -

Finding Solutions: Juliana and her friends live together for a short period of time, but they get to a point where they do not get along or agree on anything. What could they have done to rectify the situation and make it possible to stay as roommates? What rules should they have agreed on beforehand?

II. VOCABULARY WORDS: Below, write the definition for each word, either by using context clues, or by looking them up in the dictionary.

1. responsibility	6. random	11. peek
2. adjacent	7. odd	12. mentally
3. anxious	8. stretch	13. Tequila
4. adventure	9. dash	14. recover
5. grocery	10. jaw	15. smoothly

III. Use five new words from the table above to write an original sentence for each word.

1.

2.

3.

4.

5.

IV. Internet Search: Do a search on La Universidad Autónoma De Sinaloa in Mexico. Then, write a short paragraph using your own words to explain to your classmates what you have learned about this university.

Juliana from Beltrán, Mexico:
Bad Decisions

Part II

At the Universidad Autónoma De Sinaloa, I majored in Law. I attended school at night and was working at a fast food place during the day just to get by. I really didn't like working at that place much. The boss was rude, the employees were unhappy and some of the customers were very annoying and insensitive. So, I only lasted three weeks there.

After looking for a while in every newspaper, I finally found a job doing **secretarial** work in a travel agency. After a couple of weeks, my new boss, Sara seemed to be jealous of me for some reason. Every morning when I came into work, she would look at me strangely and give me a mean attitude.

I found out later that her husband had walked into the office one day and told her that I was "a beautiful new secretary." Since then, my boss became mean and jealous, according to another employee who had become my friend.

Because I wanted to avoid any kind of drama in my life, I started applying for jobs at other places. A few months later, I was offered a job at a Cola company to be a **supervisor** of production.

Even though I had no idea how I was going to do this job, I found many people in the company who guided me. Unlike my other jobs, everyone there was pleasant, and more importantly, there was no drama. I slowly learned everything I needed to know to be successful in my position.

I actually loved my job and looked forward to going to work every day, but when I started asking the director for different work schedules because I was a student, he had to let me go because he didn't think my **availability** during the day was enough, which meant that I couldn't be "completely **dedicated** to the company," according to him.

That was a very sad day for me because things were finally falling into place, and my life was back on track. I had money, my own place, and was going to school full-time, but I could lose it all if I didn't get another job soon. I became worried about not being able to pay my bills, as I was given a two-week notice to leave my job.

I had been applying for jobs everywhere for at least three weeks and started to panic because I had almost **depleted** my savings account.

One day, I was called to interview for a position in an oil company. They hired me to do **janitorial** work, such as sweeping, cleaning and other things around the office. I worked very hard, showed up early and stayed late. I really wanted to keep this job because I was tired of moving from one job to the other.

One morning, the manager asked me to come into his office to talk.

"Juliana, I have been watching you, and you have proven to me that you're very dedicated. You're also good with people. Everyone here likes you, and your positive attitude. Are you interested in changing job positions?" He asked me with a smile.

"Of course!"

"I was thinking we can put you in sales."

"Yes! Yes! I will work in sales."

"Then, you can start training tomorrow."

After one year, I had proven myself at the company and was **promoted** to the position of Department Manager. By then, I had completed my degree in Law. I just needed to find a law firm to be accepted as an **intern**.

Since interning was unpaid work, I had to have another job for a while before I **embarked** on any new **venture**. So, going back to my job at the oil company seemed like a good idea at this point. I would also be able to save enough money to come to California to visit some friends.

When I went back to see the manager of the company, he was very happy to see me.

"I hope you are here because you want to work full-time, Juliana."

"Yes, I was hoping I could go back to my old job in sales. I am available all day, every day now. I'm done with school." I told him.

For the following year, I worked six days a week and saved enough money to be able to take a little vacation to see my friends.

So, I finally made it to California that summer and stayed with my friend, Evelyn who lived with a couple of roommates.

This is where I met Eduardo, a Latino man who was twenty years older than me. I was twenty-seven at that time. Even though he seemed pleasant enough and respectful, I had told myself that I wouldn't date anyone for a long time because I had had many bad experiences dating good men who turned out to be married at the end. I didn't want to do that again.

Eduardo kept calling and **insisted** on seeing me, until one day I agreed. I guess it was kind of romantic that he wasn't giving up on me.

As the relationship became more serious, I decided to stay longer in California. I told my boss that I had a family emergency and had to stay to resolve some issues.

Eduardo made me feel safe and content. I actually saw a future with him and envisioned our having a family together.

Three weeks later, I found out I was pregnant with his baby, which complicated things for me. Now I had to make more difficult decisions. I had to think about my baby, my job back in Mexico, my future career as a lawyer and about Eduardo, who seemed very serious about our relationship.

I never thought I would run into a similar situation, but I soon discovered that Eduardo was married. In the weeks prior to confronting him, I kept asking why he was coming home late every day, and he kept giving me bogus excuses. When I did my own investigation an asked around, I was sure he was married and had been going to his other home after work almost every day.

There is absolutely nothing between me and my wife. We are going to divorce soon." Eduardo assured me when I confronted him.

So, I **reluctantly** stayed, but mostly because I was pregnant with his baby.

In order to stay busy and **contribute** to our household, I worked in a produce place Downtown Los Angeles and changed jobs often, until I had my son, Marco. It seemed like our life together was going very smoothly, and I saw some hope of settling down with Eduardo for good.

When Marco was three months old, I started asking Eduardo when he and his wife were going to start the divorce process. He would often tell me, "Soon, baby." But months went by, and the divorce didn't happen.

Eduardo began to come home late again and work longer hours on the weekends. Soon enough, I found out that his wife decided not to go through with the divorce, and Eduardo had been seeing her behind my back.

So, they got back together, and Eduardo completely **abandoned** us.

We had no support from him, financially or otherwise. To make things even more **tragic**, one year later, Eduardo went to visit his family in Mexico, and on the way there, he had a car accident, which ended in his death in 2008.

I. Writing Questions:

After reading this chapter, please go back to your annotations and write **three** WH-questions (questions that begin with what, when, where, who, which, how, how many, etc.), and **three** Yes/no questions (questions that begin with is, are, was, were, do, does, did, etc.).

WH-Questions:

1.

2.

3.

Yes/No Questions:

1.

2.

3.

Discussion Question: Juliana studies law but seems very naïve in many respects when it comes to making life decisions. Point out all instances where she made unsound decisions. Knowing Juliana's educational background, how do you think she should have handled each of those situations?

II. VOCABULARY WORDS: Below, write the definition for each word, either by using context clues, or by looking them up in the dictionary.

1. secretarial	7. intern	13. contribute
2. supervisor	8. embark	14. abandon
3. availability	9. venture	15. tragic
4. dedicated	10. morally	
5. depleted	11. insist	
6. promote	12. reluctantly	

III. Choose five words from the table above to write an original sentence for each word.

1.

2.

3.

4.

5.

IV. Internet Search: Do a search on the National Bar Exam in Mexico. Then, write a short paragraph using your own words to explain to your classmates what you have learned about this exam and whether it is different than the American Bar Exam.

Juliana from Beltrán, Mexico:
Bad Decisions

Part III

Finally, my mother was able to come and visit us in California. I had not seen her for a long time. I have to say that even though I needed my mother to be with us very badly, she could not have come a worse time. I had been cleaning houses for a while and trying to save as much money as I could so that I could take her places and show her around Los Angeles.

I tried to think of different ways to tell her about my current job but decided to just tell her the truth. I knew at that moment that I had broken my mother's heart and hoped that she would forgive me.

"You are a lawyer, not a housekeeper. What did you go to school for?" She scolded me.

Even though I didn't want to tell her about all things that happened to me up to that point in my life, I told her that I just had the worst luck trying to make a good life with my son.

"First, I'm **undocumented**, and second, I don't have good English language skills. So, I couldn't get a job that would pay well." I tried to explain, as she kept interrupting me and tried to convince me to go back with her to Mexico.

"You can try to find a job there, and I can help you take care of Marco."

"Mama, I've been here for a long time, and I don't think I can go back to living in the village. It wouldn't be fair to Marco, either." I cried.

I could tell my mom was very disappointed and sad for what had become of her daughter's life.

"What do I tell your father? This will kill him." Mom cried.

One morning after my mom had been with me for a week, she called me over to sit with her in the living room. She wanted to talk to me about "something important."

"Look, Juliana. Your father and I have been saving some money for the last few years because we wanted to help you and your sister when you got married. **Considering** the current **circumstances**, I think this is a good time to give you your share. I'll talk to your father about it first."

I was **ashamed** and **embarrassed** to have put my mom in that position, but I was also surprised to hear that my parents had any extra money saved. A while back, they stopped sending me money when I was a student, and I assumed they just didn't have it.

"Mama, you don't have to give me anything. I'll be fine. I promise."

"Juliana, please stop talking and listen to me for a few minutes. Your father and I aren't getting any younger, and I what to make sure our kids are fine."

My mom suggested the idea of purchasing a house in Los Angeles. She didn't want me to waste the money on rent anymore.

"You and Marco will have a good home, and your father and I could start visiting you both more often."

I was thinking that if my mom insisted on giving me money, I would **preferably** like to start a small business instead. My income at that time wouldn't be enough to pay for a monthly mortgage, but my mom was very **adamant** about buying a house. So, I just went along with it.

A few days later, my mom and I visited a local **realty** company to get some advice on the best way to start the process of purchasing a house. We were told that the financing company that was going to handle my loan wanted me to show that I had enough cash since I had zero credit, a low-paying job without proof of income, no bank account and no proof of having paid any taxes in previous years.

Until that point, I had no idea how much money my mom was planning to give me.

"We can show them that we have $ 20,000.00." My mom **whispered** to me, and asked me how much I had saved. "We could put all the money together to make the down payment." She continued.

What my mom didn't know was that I didn't have much.

"Mama, I'm sorry, but I only have $ 600.00 under my bed." I nervously shared with her.

Mom looked at me in disappointment again, and I could see her face turning pale.

"We can give you $ 20,000.00 now." My mom told the officer. She didn't discuss it with me at all.

I saw the finance officer write the amount down on a paper. Then she showed it to her boss and filed it away. I was expecting to get some type of document to prove that we gave the officer our money, but when my mom didn't say anything, I just kept quiet.

Later that week, the finance company asked me to give them 10,000.00 dollars more in order to bid higher on a house that we loved. Since we didn't have the money, my mom suggested that maybe we could use Sandra's share of the money and put her name on the mortgage as a co-owner.

So, Mom talked to my father and tried to convince him that it would be a good investment for all of us.

I **trusted** the people because they spoke Spanish and seemed professional enough. For those reasons, I didn't request a receipt from them again. This time, I was **supposedly** going to get the house for which I was bidding.

Weeks went by, and I wasn't in my new home. Whenever I asked the realty company about the status, they would tell me to speak to the finance officer. The finance officer would tell me that it was then in the hands of the realtor.

When things **dragged** on, and I didn't hear anything from the agents, I went and asked for my money back. The agent kept making up excuses, then offered me a **promissory note** for the amount so that I would trust them.

Yes, I had the note, but nothing changed the fact that I was not in my new home.

When I finally took the realty company to court, the judge said that the note was only signed by the realtor, and not by a **notary public**. I did not understand what that meant.

"Your honor, can I still ask for my money back?" I nervously asked.

"You need to report the company to the **Better Business Bureau** and to the police and hope that they find enough evidence to arrest whoever is in charge. Then, you can hire a lawyer and come back to court." He suggested.

Months went by, and I wasn't able to get my money back. I was told to give the case to mediation, even though it was going to take a long time if it was ever going to be resolved.

This really **devastated** me and my mom. We had no money, no house and my job as a house cleaner was not enough to pay the bills.

In the meanwhile, my mom didn't even have the strength to tell my father over the phone about the **disaster** we had created. She decided to go back to Mexico and tell him in person.

I felt horrible about what I had put my mom through. I was a lawyer and should have known better not to leave the realty office without the proper documents. I should never have trusted those people. I was **naive** to think that if they were from my country and spoke my language that they would be **trustworthy**.

This was the lowest point in my life, and I had no idea how I was going to make it better.

A friend of mine had asked me to **entertain the idea** of marrying someone who was an American citizen so that I could at least live in California legally and be able to get a good job. But, knowing my luck, I rejected the whole idea.

If I were to ever get married, I wanted to choose someone who was the right person for me. I wanted to fall in love, and not be with someone out of **convenience**.

Months went by, and I was just focused on my work and my son. Sometimes, I missed my family so much that I wanted to pack our things, get in the car and surprise my parents. What kept stopping me was the fact that my father still had not forgiven me.

Sometime before Christmas that year, I started dating Ron, who lived next door to me in my most recent apartment. Ron was generous and pleasant, and seemed to be hard-working. I would see him leave his house early with a lunch box, and then he would often come home very late.

We dated for about six months, and one evening, as I sat in my living room watching T.V. and eating dinner with my son, Ron came over. He had a beautiful bouquet of flowers and a bottle of wine.

"I'm here to ask you to marry me, and I hope you will say yes." He sounded like he had had a few drinks as his speech was slow and almost **incomprehensible**.

"Sorry. What did you say, Ron?"

"Would you marry me, Juliana?" He said it louder and clearer.

I had not thought about it at all before that day, nor had we even discussed it. I was very surprised.

Marco was watching and listening to Ron. He didn't look pleased. The only thing I could do at that time was to say, *thank you, Ron for the flowers and thank you for the proposal, but I need to think about this and talk it over with Marco and my family.*

I could see that Ron's face was turning red, and he looked a bit disappointed and even angry.

I asked him to sit down and told him that I would make him a plate of food. He whispered to me and asked if I could take Macro to the neighbor's house for a little while until we talked.

Since I felt like I embarrassed him a little, I wanted to avoid any more **awkwardness** in my son's presence. So, I took Marco to stay with my neighbor Cecilia's kids. When I came back, Ron had opened my fridge and treated himself to a beer.

"Juliana, I know I sound drunk now, and I admit I have had a few drinks, but I needed to get the courage to ask you to marry me. I have thought about this for a while, and you know we need each other."

"Ron, I'm very flattered, but I'm not ready for this **commitment**. I need to get my life in order, and I am undocumented. You know that."

"This is another reason why we should get married. You will get legal residence. Besides, we can live in one apartment rather than paying for two. I can help you take care of Marco as well."

Somehow, Ron's proposal and his promises gave me hope. So, by the end of our 30-minute conversation, I agreed to marry him, but after six months.

At first, Ron was nice and **accommodating**, even though I noticed that he drank alcohol frequently. Then, day-by-day, I realized that he was drinking too much and had become very **hostile** toward me and my son.

His actions the following weeks proved to me that he was definitely an **alcoholic.** When I mentioned sometimes that he was drinking too much, he would lie and say that it was "just a couple of beers a day," and that I was **exaggerating**.

He started hiding bottles of liquor in different places around the house. In addition, he had two troubled children who were seven and seventeen. They had been staying with their mother in a different city, but they came to stay with us every weekend. They would give us a difficult time with their **constant** demands and **unpleasant** behavior.

As if that wasn't enough, my step-sons used to steal my money and other items, and they had terrible manners. They used to throw their trash all over the house and leave their clothes anywhere they were sitting. Their bedroom was always a mess and they never showered throughout the whole weekend that they stayed with us. Also, they were very **rowdy** at the dinner table and laughed very loudly over silly and **meaningless** things. Even my young son did not think they were funny.

If I complained to Ron, he would **brush me off** and say that we had to be nice to them since we only saw them on the weekends, but they definitely **took advantage** of us. When I insisted that they should not behave the way they did, Ron would get mad at me and dismiss my concerns.

"This is my house!" He would yell.

This went on for a few months, and Ron started getting **abusive** with me, verbally and physically.

Then, I began to think of different ways to deal with him and the situation that my son and I were in, but I needed to get my legal residence papers through him. So, I forced myself to stay and act nice and happy so that Ron wouldn't change his mind about what he had promised to do for me. Even with that, his behavior became worse.

One day, Ron had been drinking all day, and when I came home, he asked me where I was.

"I was at the mall buying some clothes." I said.

"You are spending my money!" He shouted and threw a beer bottle across the living room.

I knew he was drunk, so I took my son to his room, and came back to talk to Ron nicely.

"Can I make you some dinner, my love?" I asked.

"I don't want any dinner. I want you to get the Hell out of here, you and your son!" He demanded angrily.

I asked him to take it easy, and that we should wait till the following day so that we could discuss it more, but he **insisted** that I pack my stuff and leave.

I thought for a few minutes about what I should do and where I could go and live, but I had no solution. I also didn't want to worry my mom. I tried again to be very sweet and diplomatic with him. I came closer to kiss him, but he **violently** held my hand and **twisted** my wrist. When I tried to defend myself, he started hitting me.

"Help! Help!" I screamed.

Then my son came out and jumped on him and started punching him on his face. Ron was too **exhausted** to do anything else. So, he just put his head on the pillow and fell asleep on the couch.

After that, I called the police and had Ron arrested for domestic violence. I also asked for a **restraining order**, which would be in effect for sixty days. This was to keep Ron away from me and my son until I found a way to fix my situation.

Since then, I have left Ron and found a small place for me and my son. Also, I was able to find a lawyer who helped me recover the money I lost to the realty company after years of legal battles in court. I returned the money back to my sister, Sandra, and my parents have finally forgiven me.

Now, I am in college and majoring in Child Development. After I graduate, I would like to open my own daycare business. Mostly, I want to be a good role model for my seven-year-old son and provide a good life for both of us. Unfortunately, the idea of practicing law in the U.S. seems to be far from reality, and going back to Mexico to be a lawyer would be even more difficult for me at this point. So, I have learned to accept my situation and make the best of it.

I. Writing Questions:

After reading this chapter, please go back to your annotations and write **three** WH-questions (questions that begin with what, when, where, who, which, how, how many, etc.), and **three** Yes/no questions (questions that begin with is, are, was, were, do, does, did, etc.).

WH-Questions:

1.

2.

3.

Yes/No Questions:

1.

2.

3.

- -

Idiomatic Expression: There is a saying that goes, "Fool me once, shame on you. Fool me twice, shame on me." How would you relate this idiomatic expression to what happened to Juliana and her mother? Provide evidence for your answer.

II. VOCABULARY WORDS: Below, write the definition for each word, either by using context clues, or by looking them up in the dictionary.

1. undocumented	9. devastated	18. abusive
2. realty	10. accommodate	19. insist
3. bid	11. alcoholic	20. violently
4. trust	12. constant	21. twisted
5. supposedly	13. unpleasant	22. exhausted
6. drag	14. rowdy	23. restraining order
7. promissory note	15. meaningless	24. commitment
8. Better Business Bureau	16. brush off	
	17. take advantage	

III. Choose five words from the table above to write an original sentence for each word.

1.

2.

3.

4.

5.

IV. In the table below, identify the part of speech for each word.

Word	Part of Speech (noun, verb, adjective, or adverb)
1. trust	( )
2. violently	( )
3. abusive	( )
4. insist	( )
5. supposedly	( )
6. drag	( )
7. accommodate	( )
8. bid	( )
9. undocumented	( )
10. advantage	( )
11. twisted	( )
12. exhausted	( )
13. alcoholic	( )
14. unpleasant	( )
15. commitment	( )

Xian Jun from Qingdao, China:
The Greedy Aunt

I grew up in a big city in china called, Qingdao, a major city in the east of Shandong province on the Yellow Sea of China. It is known for having the world's longest sea bridge, which is called, the Jiaozuo Bay Bridge and it connects a big urban area of Qingdao with Huang Dao district by the Jiao Zhou Bay. It is also the site of the second largest brewery in China, the Qingdao or Tsingtao Brewery, which was founded by German settlers in 1903.

I was an only child in my family. We lived in a small house, but I had my own room. It had a huge **balcony** that faced the main street. That was where I spent a lot of my time reading and watching people go by.

My friends used to come by and often jump over the balcony railing to hang out with me, but my parents did not know about it. I remember I had to stay home alone a lot, especially in the summer because my parents worked long hours. My mother had a job in a factory that **manufactured** phones for military ships, and my father was a soccer coach for two local schools.

One day, my father came home early and found some of my friends hanging out with me. I had not asked for permission. He got very upset and asked my friends to leave right away. I felt very embarrassed in front of them and ashamed that I had done something behind my father's back. He said he was worried that something bad would happen while he and my mom were at work, and that they would be held responsible.

So, he **forbade** me from letting my friends come over anymore if I was by myself. This was the biggest punishment I had ever suffered. My friends were also affected badly by my punishment because hanging out with me was their only escape from their daily boring routine at home, which was mostly studying and being closely monitored by their parents or grandparents.

I heard Mom suggesting to Dad one morning that we should move in with my **maternal** grandmother. She was living in a big house by herself at the time. I was not too excited about the idea because usually, when we went to my grandmother's house, my aunt's family would also be there, and my cousins were very rude to me.

I used to feel like a guest, but they felt more like the owners of the house. Sometimes, if I wanted to get a drink or something to eat from the fridge, one of my cousins would follow me and say, "Hey, you need to ask Grandma first." I didn't see them ask permission.

Three days later, we all drove to my grandmother's house, which wasn't very far. This time, my aunt and her family weren't there. My mom began the conversation and slowly led up to the proposal she had in mind.

My grandmother seemed agreeable, but not too excited.

"If you feel that it would benefit you and your family, I guess it's OK." Grandma slowly uttered the words.

Two weeks later, we moved in with her. **Fortunately**, I still got my own room, which was a lot more **spacious** and had a beautiful desk and chair by a window that faced the garden. The **downside** of this whole move was that I had to attend a new school and make new friends. That was not easy, but I tried my best to **acclimate** myself to the new situation.

Even though everything was great with my grandmother, and we had a good life, we still had a lot of hick-ups to get through on a daily basis. We had to be careful about how and when we moved things around the house, how much food Mom should cook, what time we all had to go to bed, and all the other **mundane** things. **Gradually**, Grandma started getting upset about everything and had many arguments with my parents, especially my father, who was extremely patient and accommodating of all her silly and unnecessary house rules and demands.

She made a big deal out of anything, and we always had drama in the house. It increasingly became **unbearable** to live there. When things **escalated** to the point of daily suffering, we decided to move out into a small apartment and save our **sanity**, or at least what was left of it.

I could not really understand why my grandmother was so angry about everything. It was like she was creating **conflicts** on purpose so that we would leave. I rattled my brain while reflecting on all the things that had happened while living with Grandma. I could not recall anything that my parents or I did to annoy or irritate her. On the contrary, we tried our best to do exactly what she asked, we kept her company and helped her with all the chores around the house. If you ask me, she could not have asked for better people to live with.

When I asked my parents why she did that, my mother explained that I was a very noisy boy and that I caused her a lot of headache.

"You misbehaved all the time and made Grandma mad."

My father had another explanation, though. He thought that my oldest aunt, Mei Lin, was **pressuring** my grandmother to make us leave because she wanted to live there and give her own house to her son, who was soon getting married.

According to my dad, Aunt Mei Lin was "a very **manipulative** and selfish woman." I heard him tell Mom one night. Mom did not agree. She blamed it all on me.

"Xian Jun just can't help himself. He annoys my mom with his noise and demands, and he **hogs** the T.V. She can't watch her regular shows or have her friends over as she did before."

I was shocked that it was all my fault.

"OK. I will not watch T.V. anymore and I will stay in my room all the time. I promise I won't bother grandma. I don't want us to move again, Mom." I begged. I could see that Mom felt bad that I had heard what she said. She hugged me and kissed me on the forehead.

"I'm sorry, son, but I am very frustrated and upset, and I'm taking it all out on you. I just can't believe what's happening here."

Not too long after that day, we moved out, and my aunt Mei Lin moved into my grandmother's house with her husband. At that time, my father was very **furious** and did not want to speak with them or have anything to do with them anymore. He decided to leave China all together and come to the U.S.A. to work.

My mother and I stayed behind so that I could finish high school.

'Once I find a job, I will bring you both to live with me." My father said.

It was a very difficult time for all of us for a while because we only had my mother's income, and I was too young to work.

My father finally got a job with a moving company, which **sponsored** him as a permanent employee. This meant that he was on a path to getting legal residence status in California. So, he continued to work hard to save money in order to provide a good home for us. He had been living in a small studio apartment near his work, but when he finally received his residence permit, he moved in to a bigger house and tried to get it furnished before we came.

In the meantime, my aunt and her family had been making my grandmother's life very difficult, as they started inviting people over and hosting dinner parties. This upset my grandmother a lot, and she felt like she was not the owner of the house anymore. She often asked my mother to pick her up to come and stay with us days at a time. I would hear her complain to my mom about my aunt, Mei Lin and her family and how greedy they were.

She would tell my mother that Aunt Mei Lin wanted her to sell the house to them. She also told her that she could try to come and live with us in the U.S. later after we had settled down. My mother would always **reject** the idea and tell her, "Mei Lin is trying to **inherit** your property while you are still alive, Mama."

My grandmother would not believe her, until one day when my aunt's husband tried to give my grandmother some money to sign over the house to him.

When my mother heard about it, she rushed over to my grandmother's house and yelled at my aunt and her husband. She **threatened** to call the police and tell them that they were trying to take advantage and force my grandmother to sign some documents.

After that, my grandmother demanded that my aunt's family leave her house and find another place to stay.

Four years had gone by, and at last, we were able to reunite with my father in the U.S. We spent the first few weeks catching up on lost time, and my father took us to all the fun places around Los Angeles. But then, unfortunately, my mother had to go back to China because she had to work one more year to get full **retirement** benefits. It was devastating for me and my father, and Mom dreaded having to go back. We were consoled that she could still live with Grandma since my aunt and her husband were no longer there, and she could save most of her money because she wouldn't have to pay for rent.

The summer was coming to an end, and I had not done anything productive. My father told me that if I wanted to enroll in a community college, I would have to live in California for a whole year before I could get any financial aid to pay for my classes. Otherwise, it was going to be costly, and I was not working yet at that time.

So, I started going to an adult School near our home to learn in the Non-Credit ESL (English as a Second Language) program, which was free for everyone.

At the school, I met a very nice Chinese girl, who became my best friend right away. She often helped pay for my food and she picked me up from home or dropped me off after school. She also studied with me and guided me throughout my stay in the school and introduced me to a good community college where she was going to attend soon.

I had found a job at an **import/export** company working in the shipping and handling department. My father used to drive me to work, and I took the bus back to the house. From there, I rode my bike to school at night.

Things were not that easy without my mother there, but my father and I managed. I was doing most of the cooking and cleaning, and he did the grocery shopping and took care of the laundry. Whatever I was paid from my job, I gave to my father because he knew how to manage money better than I could. I was hoping to save up for a car soon, since I had already **acquired** my Driver's License.

A year had passed by, and I was finally able to enroll in credit courses in college as well as get financial aid. I was now on a path to getting my education.

In my first ESL class, our professor told us about the ESL Club. She said that we could get extra credit if we attended the regular weekly meetings and volunteered sixteen hours in their **fundraising** activities.

"You need to write a paragraph about your experience every time you attend an ESL Club event." The professor said.

It sounded like a lot of work for a few extra points, but I still tried to find out more about it later and showed up to the first food sale. There, I met many new volunteers who very quickly became my friends. I enjoyed hanging out with the club board members so much that I completely forgot about the extra credit. I wanted to be there because the club was my second family on campus.

After she retired in China, my mother joined us back in the U.S. and has since found a job as a **nanny** for a Chinese family in our neighborhood. They pay her a very good salary and treat her with respect.

My father is still working for the moving company, but he doesn't do much lifting anymore, as he was recently promoted to work in the office.

As for me, I have completed my degree in business economics, and one day I want to have my own business. I feel that our life here is beginning to come together, and we are finally settling down. I only hope that one day we can restore our relationship with my grandmother and bring her here to live with us.

I. Writing Questions:

After reading this chapter, please go back to your annotations and write **three** WH-questions (questions that begin with what, when, where, who, which, how, how many, etc.), and **three** Yes/no questions (questions that begin with is, are, was, were, do, does, did, etc.).

WH-Questions:

1.

2.

3.

Yes/No Questions:

1.

2.

3.

Discussion Question: They say that some people are so greedy that they would "sell their own mother." Do you think Xian Jun's aunt and her husband are that bad? Would you justify their position of giving their house to their son and moving in with Xian Jun's grandmother to live there for free? Or, do you think they are insensitive and completely imposed themselves and took advantage of the grandmother? Either way, provide support for your answer.

II. VOCABULARY WORDS: Below, write the definition for each word, either by using context clues, or by looking them up in the dictionary.

1. balcony	11. unbearable	21. inherit
2. manufacture	12. escalate	22. threaten
3. forbid	13. sanity	23. retirement
4. maternal	14. conflict	24. import
5. fortunately	15. pressure	25. export
6. spacious	16. manipulative	26. acquire
7. downside	17. hog	27. fundraise
8. acclimated	18. furious	28. nanny
9. mundane	19. sponsor	
10. gradually	20. reject	

III. Use five words from the table above to write an original sentence for each word.

1.

2.

3.

4.

5.

IV. In the table below, identify the part of speech for each word.

Word	Part of Speech (noun, verb, adjective, or adverb)
1. balcony	( )
2. manufacture	( )
3. forbid	( )
4. fortunately	( )
5. spacious	( )
6. acclimated	( )
7. maternal	( )
8. gradually	( )
9. furious	( )
10. pressure	( )

V. Internet Search: Do a search on either the Jiao Zhou Bay Bridge or the Tsingtao Brewery in Qingdao in China. Then, write a paragraph to explain to your classmates what you have learned about either topic.

Annie from Los Angeles, U.S.A.: Alternative Education

Part I

Prayer was a big part of our daily routine in my family. My mom made sure we all prayed before each meal and before we went to sleep. She also placed a bowl of water underneath our beds "to keep **evil** things away," as she would say.

Raised in Monterey Park, California, I grew up with four siblings, three brothers and a sister. My father's family were immigrants from Mexico.

My mother was born in Guadalajara, Mexico but crossed the border with her family to come to California when she was only two years old. I have heard from some family members that it took my mom's family three long and difficult weeks to safely cross the border and make it to Los Angeles.

Both of my parents were very **religious** and committed to a local church, which we all attended every week. We later went to a church elementary school, even though it was not **accredited**. The church staff had convinced my parents and many others that it was best for their kids to be in that school away from all the drugs and harmful environment that public schools offered.

So, it was the "**alternative education**" that was going to save us from all harm out there.

The school did not have real teachers. Instead, they had church staff with either middle or high school education run the school.

We did not have a **curriculum** to follow or any **structured** lessons. We were often given a paper with some math exercises and when we were done with them, the staff would throw them in the trash. We could not ask any questions. We could just say, "Yes, Sir, No, Sir" or "Yes, Ma'am, No, Ma'am."

My parents were paying a small fee to support the church because my mother **volunteered** and helped around the church to make up for the rest of the cost. If we didn't have enough money sometimes, we donated bags of clothes, which were worth $50.00 each, and that also went toward the tuition.

Mom also spent most of her day in the school's **outreach** program, and part of her obligations was to bring kids from the inner city and help them and their families. She referred them to counselors and assisted them in registering for Bible studies in school. This way, their parents would also be committed to the church and serve there as well.

I guess you can say that our family seemed like the perfect family being regular church goers and having all their kids in a private school.

In reality, we were anything but perfect. My father suddenly left us when I was six years old. I don't remember why, and I never asked, but sometimes, he would call and say that he would someday come back.

I kept thinking about the water bowl under my bed. *Was my father evil? Is this why God is making him stay away?* So, one night, after my mom had gone to bed and my sister fell asleep, I took the water bowl out and dumped the water in the bathroom sink. I prayed that my father would come back. I kept doing this for a few nights, but nothing happened.

Since we had no income, and my mother's work at school did not pay, she had to get a real job that paid. When it was not enough, she took on another job. I was in second grade then and would see her work very hard. When she came home, she was **exhausted** and had a sad look on her face.

I felt **helpless**. All I could do was hug her and sometimes wipe off her tears. I was too young and scared to ask questions.

Things were not easy for my family at that time. I was feeling **inadequate** because I could not read or write well. My oldest brother often ran away from home, and my younger brother was always to himself in his room. Our family was falling apart.

Sometimes, we had some family members who stayed with us for one reason or another. There was this family friend who was frequently at our house. His name was Carlos and he was twenty years old. It seemed like my mom treated him as her other child.

I must have been about eight and a half years old when Carlos used to come to my room and sleep in my bed. He would pretend to read me stories. Then he would touch my body and tell me to just stay quiet.

I was very scared and couldn't tell anyone. Carlos said that he would hurt me and my family if I told on him. So, I kept it to myself for months, but Carlos started to ask me to do things that I didn't want to do. I tried to put a bigger bowl of water under my bed, but Carlos kept hurting me, more and more each time.

I was about nine years old when Carlos finally disappeared. My mom tried to look for him and was actually worried about him. I was still very scared to tell her what had happened.

That period of my life was very dark and depressing. I was going through a lot of pain and **suffering**, and my own mother, who was also **struggling** with many issues, was counseling other kids.

From the age of eight to ten, I had only learned basic math skills like addition, subtraction and some multiplication. We had no science or history. We had no art or music. If we asked about how something was made or created, they would tell us that it was God's work.

The school was like a **prison** with a bunch of uneducated people telling us what to do and making us feel **guilty** for everything we did or didn't do. They even convinced our parents that kids needed more discipline.

So, they took it upon themselves to hit us with a **wooden** stick and punish us in different ways. This was, of course, with the knowledge of our parents. Still, my mother and **siblings** had to keep the image of a perfect family, always smiling and always helping other people in need.

In sixth grade, I hated myself and became **suicidal**. People thought I was very smart because of my ability to **articulate** well. I was trying very hard to show an image that I was not able to uphold.

Around this time of my life is when my dad decided to come back into our lives. Just like I never asked why he left, I never asked why he came back. I was just thinking that maybe the bigger water bowl under my bed kept Carlos away and brought my father back.

Dad tried his best to spend quality time with us. He was very loving and **encouraging**. He would often hug me and tell me he loved me before he went to work and when he came back. It felt safe having my father back.

I. Writing Questions:

After reading this chapter, please go back to your annotations and write **three** WH-questions (questions that begin with what, when, where, who, which, how, how many, etc.), and **three** Yes/no questions (questions that begin with is, are, was, were, do, does, did, etc.).

WH-Questions:

1.

2.

3.

Yes/No Questions:

1.

2.

3.

Discussion Question: Annie's elementary school as part of the "alternative education" system seems to be very corrupt and inefficient and well as ineffective. Also, teachers do not have the minimum qualifications to teach. Do you think these schools should still operate to provide an alternative to traditional education or should they be closed down? Please provide support for your answer.

II. VOCABULARY WORDS: Below, write the definition for each word, either by using context clues, or by looking them up in the dictionary.

1. alternative	8. volunteer	15. struggle
2. raised	9. outreach	16. prison
3. religious	10. exhausted	17. guilty
4. accredited	11. helpless	18. wooden
5. alternative education	12. inadequate	19. sibling
	13. molest	20. suicidal
6. curriculum	14. suffer	21. encouraging
7. structured		

III. Use five new words from the table above to write an original sentence for each word.

1.

2.

3.

4.

5.

IV. In the table below, identify the part of speech for each word.

Word	Part of Speech (noun, verb, adjective, or adverb)
1. volunteer	( )
2. sibling	( )
3. struggle	( )
4. encourage	( )
5. outreach	( )
6. guilty	( )
7. suicidal	( )
8. depression	( )
9. extremely	( )
10. lecture	( )

V. Internet Search: Do a search on what are the necessary credentials that teachers have to possess in order to teach in K-12 schools in California. Then, write a paragraph to explain to your classmates what you have learned about the topic.

Annie from Los Angeles, U.S.A.:
Alternative Education

Part II

In seventh grade, teachers noticed that I was not strong in any area. So, they wanted me to repeat sixth grade. I strongly **refused**.

We decided as a family that we were all better off doing home schooling. That did not go well for me either since we had no oversight or supervision. We sat there watching DVDs of boring **lectures** without any interaction.

My younger brothers and sisters seemed to do well, though. They would always complete the work and mail it in, but I lagged behind.

Depression then hit me hard, and I hated myself even more. I did not want to ask for help, nor did I let anyone into my life.

As I became very **bitter** about everything, my mother started pushing me to get back into school. She said that I should never rely on anyone, and to be responsible for my own life. On the other hand, I thought at that time that I would never be college material. It was only a dream that I would ever enter a university.

One day, my mother became very **frustrated** with me and my lack of motivation that she **slapped** me on the face and said, "If you don't go back to school, you will end up three hundred pounds, alone and living somewhere under a bridge."

Her harsh words kept playing in my head, and I started eating less and less after that. I would eat in front of my family and later force myself to vomit. I became **bulimic** and spent most of my time in my room. I was tired and looked **malnourished**. Then my hair started falling out.

When people asked why I was not eating well, I would them that I had become **vegan**. This shut them up for a while, but things became worse for me when I had no energy to do anything except sleep.

My parents then **forced** me to see a doctor who had been **anorexic** herself. I trusted her and told her that since I had failed everything else, I only had control of my weight. I wanted to at least look perfect. She then referred me to a therapist who specialized in eating disorders.

After many sessions with the **therapist**, I was pushed by my parents to go back to school. This time, I went to a public high school in the area. I had to take an **assessment** test since I had been away from school for a couple of years.

Even though I placed in seventh grade math and English, they still accepted me in twelfth grade.

For the first time in my life, I walked into a real classroom with a real teacher who had teaching **credentials**. There was **interaction** in the classroom, and I loved how the teacher called on me many times. I felt very smart, and people actually thought I was a **nerd**. I felt alive for the first time in my life. I was **eager** to complete high school and maybe go to college after.

I wanted to follow my dream of becoming a piano teacher.

I moved away to San Jose, California to a Christian college and majored in music. One thing they did not know was the fact that I had never taken a piano lesson in my life.

One teacher called me to her office and told me, "there must be something else you could be good at, but music is not it for you."

I was heartbroken. I wanted to make my mother proud because since I was little, I had been telling her that this was my dream. She was paying a lot of money for me to be in this school, and I had let her down.

After my failure, I came back home and got a job at a department store, but my parents wanted me to go to college. I had heard about a community college nearby. People in our church said horrible things about it, so we wouldn't go there, but I took a chance and enrolled there anyway. I took a couple of classes and loved the school, the teachers and many students who became my close friends.

I had always been **fascinated** with the Chinese culture, architecture and language, so I took a Chinese class where I learned about teaching English abroad.

This was what I wanted to do for the rest of my life.

Then I met some international students who were members of the ESL Club (English as a Second Language Club). I heard their stories of how they felt **homesick**, lonely and out of place when they first came to California.

I learned that some of them were under a lot of pressure to do well because their parents would be upset if they did not. I learned that some of them get sick or sometimes do not do well, but they are afraid to tell their families or talk to someone because of **embarrassment**. This made me very sad.

On the other hand, their stories **inspired** me very much because even with the language barrier and all the pressure that was placed on them, the majority of those students **strive** for "As," and most of them want to go to the best universities.

I wanted to do the same. "If they can do it with no family around to support them, and with limited English, then I have no excuse." I told myself.

I have graduated from a university with a BA in English and plan to teach in China for a year before I start my career in California.

I. Writing Questions:

After reading this chapter, please go back to your annotations and write **three** WH-questions (questions that begin with what, when, where, who, which, how, how many, etc.), and **three** Yes/no questions (questions that begin with is, are, was, were, do, does, did, etc.).

WH-Questions:

1.

2.

3.

Yes/No Questions:

1.

2.

3.

Discussion Question: Annie's family decide to have all their kids do home schooling. This does not go well at all for Annie as she could not complete the packets on time, and the curriculum was very boring. What is your opinion about home schooling? Home schooling is not for everyone, but what do you think could be some of the advantages or disadvantages of this type of education?

II. VOCABULARY WORDS: Below, write the definition for each word, either by using context clues, or by looking them up in the dictionary.

1. refuse	10. therapist	18. fascinated
2. lecture	11. assessment	19. homesick
3. depression	12. malnourished	20. embarrassment
4. bitter	13. vegan	21. inspire
5. frustrated	14. force	22. strive
6. slap	15. interaction	
7. bulimic	16. nerd	
8. anorexic	17. eager	
9. credentials		

III. In the table below, identify the part of speech for each word.

Word	Part of Speech (noun, verb, adjective, or adverb)
1. inspire	( )
2. anorexic	( )
3. encouraging	( )
4. fascinated	( )
5. assessment	( )
6. homesick	( )
7. therapist	( )
8. interaction	( )
9. strive	( )
10. force	( )

IV. ONLINE SEARCH: Find a current short newspaper article on Alternative Education, Anorexia or Bulimia. Read the article, annotate it and summarize it in your own words in a short paragraph to explain to your classmates what you have learned about the topic you chose. Go to http://www.latimes.com and use the key words, alternative education, Anorexia, or Bulimia to do your search.

GUIDELINES FOR AN ARTICLE SUMMARY:

- In an article summary, we first need to identify the **main idea**. So, we ask ourselves why this article was written and published. In addition, clues like the title, the place it was published, the date, the kind of article, and repeated notions can also help us determine the main idea.
- We need to read the article several times so that in the first reading we can get the **gist**[1] of the article.
- While reading the second or third time, write down any important information that may give you the **general notion**[2] of the article because that will be the **thesis**[3] for your summary.
- In your summaries, you should clearly state the main idea of the author, use your own words, make the summary a lot shorter than the original article, explain the main arguments, and add some supporting details. **Do not include your opinion.**

EXAMPLE OF HOW TO BEGIN A SUMMARY:

In the article, "Teenage Problems" by Dr. Dennis McCormick, from the *Los Angele Times,* retrieved on January 5, 2018, the author states that …

---

[1] **gist:** central theme or the heart of the matter
[2] **general notion:** general idea
[3] **thesis:** an argument or a belief

Keyman from Foshan, China:
Life after Regret

"Keyman" is a nickname I was given by my landlord when I came to the USA. I was born in a big city called, Foshan in the southern part of China, which is known for producing some of the most beautiful ceramics in the world, as my grandfather used to tell me. It is also the home of the Cantonese version of the Chinese Opera, in addition to Kung Fu, a type of martial art and the lion dance, which is a traditional dance not only in the Chinese culture, but also in other Asian countries. My father says that mimicking the lion's movement can bring good luck and big fortunes. I don't know about that, though.

My parents and I lived in a small humble home in a semi-good neighborhood. My father was a civil engineer and my mother was a part-time saleswoman at a company that **manufactured** knives. She stayed home for the most part to take care of me. I was the only child in the family.

Even though my parents wanted to have more children, the one-child policy in China kept them from doing so. Otherwise, if they had other children, they would have to pay a big fine, which they could not afford. They decided that they would put all their energy on getting me into good schools.

As a child, I was very shy and not much of a social kid. So, primary school was boring, and I did not make many friends. After school, my parents were too busy working, and as a result, I ended up spending a lot of time with my grandfather, who also lived in Foshan just a few miles from our house. My grandmother had passed away three years **prior**.

My grandfather tried his best to keep me **entertained** when I was with him, but I was just not interested in anything around the house, and he was too old to take me out anywhere.

I wished that I had a brother or sister, or even any cousins who lived near us, but the cousins I had lived in Beijing. We only saw each other when there were big events, such as weddings or funerals.

In junior high, my parents enrolled me in a boarding school where I would spend five days in school. At first, it was not easy because I did not know anyone, and my family was far. But soon, I became very close with my roommates, and we depended on each other when we felt homesick or needed help with our homework. They were basically my family away from home.

When my parents used to come on the weekends to pick me up, I really did not want to go home anymore. I was having a lot of fun with my friends, and we had our own space and a structure that we all got used to.

One weekend, I asked my parents not to come and pick me up because I was not feeling that well and just wanted to rest in my dorm room. They were worried about me, or they got **suspicious** and wondered what I was up to at school. Without telling me, they came to my school anyway and surprised me.

I was happily playing basketball with my friends who had decided to do the same thing and tell their parents they were not feeling well either. When my father saw me having fun, he was very angry, and my mother took it **personally**.

"Please pack your stuff and come to the car!" My father demanded.

"Father, can I please stay here this weekend?" I **begged**.

"I asked you to pack your things and get in the car, son." He shouted.

On the way home, I received a long lecture about the importance of family, and how we should never forget our parents and what they do for us.

That day, I felt very guilty. I did not say anything to my parents the rest of the way.

That same night, my grandfather got very sick. So, I was left alone in the house while my parents took Grandpa to the hospital. Before he left, Grandpa told me that he was proud of me and that when he felt well enough, he was going to visit me at school.

On the other hand, all night, I was thinking, "I could have stayed in the dorm with my friends. This is going to be a very boring weekend."

In the morning, my parents came home without my grandfather. They informed me that he had died of **Pneumonia**. I just could not **comprehend** what they had just said.

"What do you mean he died? What is Pneumonia?"

"Your grandfather had a viral infection of some sort last week and had not fully recovered. The doctor said that his lungs were inflamed due to bacteria or a viral infection." Mother explained.

Not wanting to believe what had just happened, I kept asking questions.

"What is Pneumonia anyway?"

"If you are really interested in knowing more about what killed your grandfather, then go look it up." My father snapped angrily.

He was still upset with me. Of course, I did not dare say anything back. I went to my room and thought about all the memories I had of my grandfather, and all the things he used to do with me.

One memory kept playing in my head over and over. It was the time he and I had walked to the neighborhood park. My grandfather was breathing heavily and suggested that we go back home so that he could take some medicine, but I insisted that we stay because I had made a couple of friends at the park and wanted to continue playing.

I left him sitting on the bench and went back to my new friends. Suddenly, I saw a bunch of people gathering around him, and somebody was yelling, "Call an ambulance! Call an ambulance!"

When the ambulance car came, I was afraid of staying behind by myself. So, I went and told the **paramedics** that the old man was my grandfather.

Riding in the back of the ambulance car with my grandfather, I felt bad and even **ashamed** that I had **insisted** to stay at the park even when he was begging me to go. I was selfish then, and now I felt even more selfish

98

and guilty for not having spent much time with him in the previous two or three years.

I finally gathered myself and came out of my room. Mom was **slouching** sadly on the sofa, and Dad was sitting in his chair **staring** at the wall. I saw how sad he was because we lost my grandmother when I was only two years old and now my father had lost both parents. It was years before my father was able to smile again.

After I graduated from junior high, my friends and I decided to try and **convince** our parents to enroll us in the same boarding school so that we would stay close. They all agreed. We were six friends and lived in three rooms next to each other.

We had the same classes, we did our homework together, and we enjoyed the same sports. Those were the years when we all learned to be **independent**.

We had less supervision than in junior high and most of us did not see our parents as often as before. In fact, one time I stayed three months without going home. We had to study a lot, and this could not be done at home, as we studied in groups.

I liked the feeling of being on my own and no longer was I shy. I also learned how to get along with others and follow school rules. I later became the person in charge of **keeping a tab** on students who did not follow rules, like not wearing a uniform or not taking naps on time or showing up to group study sessions.

I was also doing very well in school and made many new friends, especially when I did not turn them into the administration for breaking rules. Having this kind of power actually made me popular at school.

Before I even graduated from high school, my parents had been discussing the idea of my coming to the USA to continue my education. They said that in China, I would not have many opportunities, and that the environment there was no longer **suitable.** I was very excited about **venturing out**, especially to the U.S.A.

After we graduated in 2012, one of my friends and I got our papers together through an agency that charged us a fee for filling out all the forms and sending them to a community college in California. We were both accepted to the same ESL (English as a Second Language) program.

When we arrived, we stayed in a hotel and were searching on the Internet for a house to rent. Luckily, we found a place near the college. It was a very nice one-bedroom house. We registered for some classes and made many friends right away.

I used to hear about how difficult it was when people first arrived in the USA, but my friend and I felt very comfortable upon arrival.

The professors were very helpful, classes were available, and we loved our house. To make things even better, we learned about some clubs on campus and joined a couple of them.

This has been the best experience of my life. I am glad my parents put me in boarding schools because I feel the experience prepared me to be a responsible and independent person, and I can handle many situations on my own.

By the way, if you wondered at all why I was given the name, "Keyman," our landlord, Mr. Clark gave me the house key the day we moved in. I asked for another key for my friend, but Mr. Clark said, "Well, I only have one. So, you are the Keyman for now, until you can have another one made." From then on, I chose to be called Keyman.

I. Writing Questions:

After reading this chapter, please go back to your annotations and write **three** WH-questions (questions that begin with what, when, where, who, which, how, how many, etc.), and **three** Yes/no questions (questions that begin with is, are, was, were, do, does, did, etc.).

WH-Questions:

1.

2.

3.

Yes/No Questions:

1.

2.

3.

Reflection: in this story, Keyman greatly regrets not having spent much time with his grandfather and for lying to his parents. Think about a time when you did something you were not proud of. Looking back, what could you have done differently to avoid regret? Also, have you resolved or rectified the situation related to that issue since then?

II. VOCABULARY WORDS: Below, write the definition for each word, either by using context clues, or by looking them up in the dictionary.

1. manufacture	8. comprehend	14. convince
2. prior	9. paramedics	15. independent
3. entertain	10. ashamed	16. keep a tab
4. suspicious	11. insist	17. suitable
5. personally	12. slouch	18. venture out
6. beg	13. stare	
7. pneumonia		

III. Use five new words from the table above to write an original sentence for each word.

1.

2.

3.

4.

5.

IV. Internet Search: You have three choices. Do a search on Pneumonia, and its causes and effects, search the martial art, Kung Fu, or the Lion Dance. Then, write a paragraph using your own words to explain to your classmates what you have learned on any of the three topics.

V. In the table below, identify the part of speech for each word.

Word	Part of Speech (noun, verb, adjective, or adverb)
1. manufacture	( )
2. prior	( )
3. entertain	( )
4. suspicious	( )
5. personally	( )
6. beg	( )
7. selfish	( )
8. ashamed	( )
9. insist	( )
10. personally	( )

Christine from Jakarta, Indonesia: Poor, But Not Miserable

I must have read a thousand books by the time I was eighteen. I used to read anytime I had an opportunity because it was how I escaped all life's daily problems. Mom used to call me, **"a bookworm."**

Most of the books I read were **Manga**, which are Japanese comics that are translated into many languages. I would get lost in the stories, and the **graphics** kept me flipping pages. My favorite **genres** were action-adventure and **mystery**.

I would sometimes draw pictures of different things in the blank pages of the books. One day, Mom saw me drawing and said, "You are an amazing artist, honey!" She exaggerated a bit, but somehow, she **encouraged** me to take this hobby to the next level.

"You should start looking for a good arts school." Mom suggested.

"It's too soon, mom." I told her.

I had already thought about what my major was going to be in college. I wanted to be a graphic designer, as I loved drawing and the world of Manga. I imagined myself writing and **illustrating** comic books and becoming famous one day like the Japanese author and illustrator, Masashi Kishimoto, who wrote the popular series, *Naruto* or Takeshi Obata and Tsugumi Ohba, who wrote the series, *Death Note*.

I was born in Jakarta, the capital and the largest city in Indonesia. It is situated in the northwest of Java Island. It is known as the most **populous** city in all of East Asia, but it is a place where people from all over the world come to have a great time. The nightlife is always exciting and the people there are very friendly and hospitable. I consider myself lucky to have been born and raised there.

I was raised only by my mother. My parents were married for a short while, and when my mother found out she was pregnant, apparently, my father left for reasons that I still don't know.

I asked my mother where my father was when I was five years old, and I was **slapped** on the face. After that, I never **dared** to ask her.

I grew up an only child, and my mother worked very hard to provide a good life for me. She worked as a school bus driver for years. Taking on the roles of both parents, she had no life of her own. We lived in a tiny apartment, which did not have a **stove**. So, we never really cooked anything at home.

We knew a lady in the neighborhood who cooked **meals** for others. The lady cooked dinner for us every day and was paid monthly. We did have a microwave oven and used it to heat up food and hot water. As for the laundry, my mother did it all by hand every Saturday. I would sometimes help her hang the big pieces out to dry.

My mother usually worked long hours and was not home until 8:00 PM every night. Because of that, after school, I would take the bus home and stay by myself doing homework, reading Manga books, and sometimes, I watched television.

Twice a week, I went to see a math tutor because Mom did not want me to have any bad grades in any subject, and math was my least favorite subject. The tutor was kind of nice, and his mother would always have a hot cup of tea ready for me when I arrived at their house. I think she was trying to encourage students to come back for more lessons. Her son was making a lot of many giving private math lessons.

In general, I really had no major **complaints** in my life. I was fine doing my own thing and enjoying my freedom, but my mother started feeling **guilty** about leaving me alone at home for long hours every day. So, after changing many jobs, she finally settled for a job in a local real estate company.

She had heard from some of her close friends that she could make a lot of money in that field. I think Mom could have done well in any field. She was a **hustler** and very much business-minded.

Mom became very good at what she did that she decided, with her partners, to start their own company. By the time I was ready to enter high school, my mother had already saved enough money to buy the apartment in which we lived. I started seeing her more at home, and she was finally a happy woman.

Sometimes I wished I would get the **courage** to ask her about my father, but I was always afraid to open up the subject and **ruin** her happiness. I really wanted to know what had happened between them. I wondered about what kind of person my father was, who my grandparents were and many other things that ran through my mind, but I never asked. *"Maybe one day when Mom thought I was **mature** enough, she would tell me herself about what had happened."* I would tell myself.

As months went by and between reading books and hanging out with my friends in high school, I forgot all about my father and tried to enjoy my life as much as I could.

Sometimes my mom would see that I was bored or **preoccupied**, and she would tell me, "I need to find you some place where you can learn some new skills."

She tried to enroll me in many after school activities so that I would "be better prepared for college," according to her. She spent most of her money on me and my **extracurricular** activities. I wish I could tell you that I enjoyed any of them, but I did not. Nevertheless, I made the best out of those situations and tried to have fun as not to **disappoint** Mom.

One day after I graduated from high school, Mom came to me and said, "Christine, you need to start preparing for the **TOEFL** (Test of English as a Foreign Language)," which people take if they wanted to study in the U.S.A.

I was surprised because we had never talked about it. It seemed as if I had no choice because whatever questions I asked, and whenever I **protested**, she told me that it was for my own good, and that she had already made the decision.

I tried to tell my mother that I was thinking of going to a design school and that I had many friends that I would leave behind, but she would not hear of it.

"You have to go to the U.S.A. and stay with your aunt. I will pay for everything." She yelled loudly from the bedroom.

"I don't want to stay with my aunt. I won't feel comfortable." I cried.

"You don't need to worry about anything except your school." she would repeatedly say. "You should be happy and grateful that you are getting this opportunity, Christine. Many girls your age would do anything to have the same chance."

After going back and forth and arguing together for a few days, Mom found me a place to take all kinds of preparation courses. I was doing that there for six months. Soon after that, I passed the TOEFL test. All that time, I was having mixed feelings about the whole idea of going to study abroad.

I wondered why my mother suddenly wanted to send me to America. *"Does she have a boyfriend or something? Is she getting married?"*

I was also **secretly** excited. The more I read about studying abroad, the more interested I became. I thought of it as a new adventure, and if it did not work out, I could always come back to Jakarta.

My aunt and her daughter, who lived in the U.S.A., helped get me accepted to a community college ESL program near their home where it was a walking distance.

I got my visa and ticket within a couple of months and was going to travel in an airplane for the first time in my life. I was very scared, but extremely **anxious** for the new experience. It took us fourteen hours to arrive to Los Angeles where my aunt and cousin would be waiting.

Unfortunately, I was held in **Customs** for three hours without **access** to call my relatives. When I finally came out, I could not wait to see my aunt. She had flowers and balloons for me, and my cousin gave me a little stuffed animal with some candy. I had seen my cousin a couple of times in the past when she would go to Indonesia to visit my maternal grandparents. She seemed very nice and welcoming.

At first, things were going very well. My cousin and her friends took me to all the popular theme parks and we went to the movies and even to a Beyoncé concert. All those things were new experiences to me, and I was enjoying every minute. But, soon after that, my cousin was trying to convince me to change my major from animation to business. It was as if she was on a **mission**.

"You will not be able to find a good-paying job drawing cartoon characters. You are not that good anyway." She said to me many times.

I could not understand where she was coming from. Why was she so concerned about my future job all of a sudden? Why didn't my aunt speak to me about this subject? This issue bothered me a lot, but since I was living with them, I tried to be as **diplomatic** as I could.

"My mom and I have already discussed this, and she agreed with me." I told my cousin softly.

"I don't think your mom knows what it takes to live in California, to study and to have your own place one day." My cousin replied, almost angrily.

I began to think that she was trying to convince me to major in something that would guarantee me a good job so that I would be able to move out and get my own place.

I guess she had not been happy about the idea of my staying there because she had to share her bedroom with me. I did not **blame** her, but my mom was sending my aunt money every month to pay for my expenses and school fees and supplies. She was actually sending them more money than I needed, but I had to almost beg for money every time I needed it for something.

This affected our relationship and living there became very uncomfortable. I did not want to bother my mom about all these issues, so I kept it to myself for a while.

One day as I was doing my homework, my cousin came into the bedroom and asked me, "Are you going to change majors or what?"

She threatens that if I didn't change my major, she would have her mom send me back home. I got very angry because she was able to make her own decision about her major but wanted to control what I did with my life.

I finally called my mother and told her about the situation. She did not act upset, but soon after that call, my cousin became very nice to me.

"Wow! Did you draw this?" My cousin saw one of my drawings on the bed one evening. "You are getting better, I think." She added.

I did not know at that time what my mom said to my aunt and cousin, but things started to improve in terms of the day-to-day routine.

One day when I called my mom on the phone, I asked her what she had done or said to my aunt.

"Not much. I just offered to send more money per month. Money can solve a lot of problems, my dear." Mom said.

I was happy and disappointed to hear that.

During my second semester in college, I joined the ESL Club and started going to their regular weekly meetings. I had a lot of fun and met more people from all over the world. I also met the advisor who was a full-time ESL professor.

In one of the meetings, I was listening to the Board members talking about an upcoming fundraiser and decided to **doodle** some drawings on a piece of paper. The advisor happened to be walking around the room and saw what I was doing.

"Very nice! You are very talented, my friend." She smiled at me and whispered, "Could I see you after the meeting?"

I did not know whether I was in trouble for drawing when I should have been listening or she wanted to talk to me about my art. I was nervous for the rest of the meeting and my mind went to a million places.

After the meeting was over, the advisor motioned for me to follow her across the way to her office to talk. On the way there, we introduced ourselves to each other. As soon I as we sat down, she asked me, "Would you be interested in **illustrating** a book that I have been writing? It is a collection of short stories based on my **character** as a teen ager growing up on a farm in Syria."

I was surprised, and suddenly, memories from childhood **rushed** to my head.

"Of course, I am interested," I thought.

Yes, I have always dreamt of writing and illustrating my own book, but this was a great opportunity to start somewhere.

"Do you think I am good enough to illustrate in books? I asked. "I only draw cartoons." I added.

"Well, you can draw me some samples of the main characters in my book. I will describe the **physical appearance** of each character, and you can try to match the description I have in mind. We will go from there. What do you think?" She smiled.

The next day, I brought her my **samples**. I had worked on them all night long. I was hoping she would like them and give me the job because I wanted to prove to my aunt and cousin that I was good enough and that I take my work seriously. Plus, the extra money would help me buy a new laptop.

"This is amazing, Christine!" the advisor was very pleased with the results.

"Can you draw in **3D**?" she asked.

"Yes, I can. I will do one right now."

Within a month, the book was **published**, and my name was on the cover as the illustrator. I was very proud of myself. I ordered ten copies to show all my family members, especially those who did not believe in me or my **talent**.

Six months later, the same professor asked me to illustrate another book, a **sequel** to the first. I was able to use these experiences on my **resume**, and from there, my mind was **solidly** set on majoring in Animation Design.

Down the road, I learned about a program where you could train to be a professor's assistant through the ESL Club. Students were trained in the use of smart classroom equipment and computer skills in order to assist some ESL professors. Right away, I signed up for the training. I had to **shadow** another assistant a few times to make sure I knew how to handle the smart classroom equipment and whatever other tasks professors required me to complete.

Once I felt ready, I asked one of my former professors if she needed an assistant.

"What do you mean?" She asked.

I showed her my certificate of completion, and she was surprised that a program like that existed.

"I need to know who the director of this program is so that I know who to talk to if there are any issues." She **asserted**.

I knew the job did not pay anything, but it was still considered work experience. Besides, I would be able to spend more time in an ESL classroom and improve my English language skills. It was a win-win situation for me. The professor contacted me the following afternoon and told me I could start my new job in a week. I could not wait to tell my mom and my aunt's family.

I continued to be the professor's assistant for three semesters and had the chance to meet many people on campus. In addition, I volunteered with both, the Anime and the ESL Club. This gave me the opportunity to help students and practice speaking English. Along the way, I learned new skills while networking with students, staff and faculty in many disciplines.

The following semester, I was elected Vice-President of the ESL Club. This has been the most rewarding experience of my college life. The friends I made then are still my best friends till now. We do everything together and we support one another in every way. We have created our own family away from home, which makes our lives a lot easier, since we do not see our families very often.

Last year, I graduated with a BA in Animation Design and have worked with two major companies, but because I am an international student, both companies had to let me go. I am still looking for my dream job, but I continue to seek opportunities to learn new things and to help others as much as I can. I love where I am right now, and I am looking forward to new endeavors in the future.

I. Writing Questions:

After reading this chapter, please go back to your annotations and write **three** WH-questions (questions that begin with what, when, where, who, which, how, how many, etc.), and **three** Yes/no questions (questions that begin with is, are, was, were, do, does, did, etc.).

WH-Questions:

1.

2.

3.

Yes/No Questions:

1.

2.

3.

Discussion Question: Christine's mother decides that her daughter will come to the USA to study and live with her aunt after graduating from high school. She does not consult with Christine about the decision. We often hear the expression, "parents know better." Do you think it has worked out for the better in Christine's case? Provide support for your answer.

II. VOCABULARY WORDS: Below, write the definition for each word, either by using context clues, or by looking them up in the dictionary.

1. bookworm	13. guilty	25. customs
2. graphics	14. hustler	26. access
3. genre	15. courage	27. mission
4. mystery	16. ruin	28. diplomatic
5. encourage	17. mature	29. blame
6. illustrate	18. preoccupied	30. influence
7. slap	19. extracurricular	31. doodle
8. populous	20. disappoint	
9. dare	21. protest	
10. stove	22. secretly	
11. meal	23. anxious	
12. complaint	24. unfortunately	

III. Use five new words from the table above to write an original sentence for each word.

1.

2.

3.

4.

5.

IV. In the table below, identify the part of speech for each word.

Word	Part of Speech (noun, verb, adjective, or adverb)
1. preoccupied	( )
2. extracurricular	( )
3. disappoint	( )
4. protest	( )
5. illustrate	( )
6. populous	( )
7. blame	( )
8. diplomatic	( )
9. secretly	( )
10. anxious	( )

V. Internet Search: Do a search on the city of Jakarta to find out more information about what it is popular for, what major famous hotels and building structures are located there and other important aspects. Then, write a short paragraph using your own words to explain to your classmates what you learned about its population, what products the city produces, what it imports or exports, and its tourism.

Lin from Beijing, China:
Music in My Blood

I have loved music ever since my mother used to sit me next to her at the kitchen table as she cooked and listened to her favorite radio station. I must have been two years old when she helped me memorize **dozens** of songs. Until now, those memories are among the **fondest** from my childhood.

I was born in the province of Beijing, the capital of China. This is the city that was chosen to be the home of the emperor. It is famous for its elaborate and massive palaces, temples and gardens as well as many parks and tombs.

In Beijing, you will also find **skyscrapers** in an area called, Zhong Guan Cun, which is often called Silicon Valley because it is a hub for the latest technologies and **innovations**.

As I grew older, my parents enrolled me in music and singing lessons. This continued throughout my years in secondary school. My interest in all types of music grew and grew. I used to eat, sleep, dream and drink music.

So, many years ago after I had graduated from high school, I had a dream of becoming a music **compiler** at a popular radio station in the city of Beijing, China. I wanted to play the most beautiful music to a **devoted audience,** like my mother.

At that time, many people I knew in our circle of friends wanted to work in a radio station, so the competition was **fierce**. I was **determined** to **overcome** this difficulty and make my dream come true. The first thing I had to do to qualify and have an edge over other candidates was to pass a **comprehensive** exam. So, I started to seriously study for this exam in the spring of 1988.

In order to do well on the exam, I had to move to Tianjin City and enroll in a specialized program, which was going to be very costly for my family. My parents were very poor, but I was determined to go after my goal. I told my parents that the program was free, and all I needed was a few hundred dollars for the trip and the textbooks. Of course, I was lying.

When I arrived at the music school in Tianjin, I still had my suitcase with me because I really had no place to stay. I figured that there could be some dorm rooms on campus, but that was not the case. The program director **guided** me to an office where I could be assisted in finding a room to rent or share.

There was a family who had a big house near the school and rented out rooms to students. I paid for the first month, but the landlord asked for a deposit of $200.00, which I did not have.

"I am planning to work right away and pay you. I promise. I am a hard-working **individual** and will not disappoint you." I told Mr. Chen.

Somehow, the landlord's wife asked him to trust me.

"We can hold his passport or ID until he pays." The wife suggested.

I could see that she was a lot more compassionate that her husband. She even offered me some dinner and gave me a bag of snacks for later. The room was nice enough, but the window faced an ally that was full of garbage bins. This certainly was not a good source of inspiration.

The next morning, I walked back to the school to see about my classes and the cost per semester. According to the program director, I needed to complete some courses in **contemporary** literature, classical literature, electronics, advanced math, engineering math and journalism. Yes, I needed to be **knowledgeable** in all those areas if I wanted to pass the exam.

At first, I did not have the money for tuition or for books. So, for the first semester, I did not attend school. Instead, I got a job in a local factory to pay for my expenses. I also saved enough money to buy a bike **to get around** and was able to go to school in the evening.

It took me about two hours to get to school by bike, but I managed. Sometimes it was very difficult to be on a bike, especially when the weather was cold or rainy, which was very **discouraging**. So, I used to tell myself that it was a **temporary** situation and it would pass.

Day by day, I was able to get through it alright. When the weather was nice, I felt **energized**, motivated and hopeful and used to study all night without feeling tired. Believe me! I took advantage of every minute during the nice weather and produced as much as **humanly** possible.

In the meanwhile, my parents were regularly getting updates from me. "Things are great here." I would always tell my mother, who was very worried I was not eating well. I used to send them pictures of me and my classmates.

"You look so skinny, my dear son." Mom would always tell me on the phone.

"No. No. I eat healthy food and exercise regularly." I would answer her. "The landlord's wife always feeds me and the other students." I would add.

Working during the day and studying in the evening for four years, I finally passed all my courses with excellent grades. I focused so much on learning math, and yes, math and music are very much connected. I also put in many hours of practice and saw tutors whenever I could, until I became **remarkably** good in every subject.

In the spring of 1992, I was able to pass the exam and was hired right after to work at the Tianjin Radio station in China. I held the position of a compiler for FM Music City Program. I combined Chinese **folk** music with popular culture and served a wide audience at that time.

My mother switched from her regular radio station and waited all day for me to come on so that she could hear my voice. Sometimes she would call me and request certain songs to be played on the air. They were songs to which she and I used to listen.

Right now, I am in the U.S. trying to start a new life with my family and I know the road will be difficult, but compared to the road I had taken in the past, this is going to be smooth sailing. Even though music is still in my blood and would love to have a job that would allow me to do what I love, I have decided to take English courses in a community college to learn the language so that I can be better prepared when I start looking for a new job. It could be in the music industry or anything else. The idea is that I am not afraid of doing something new. So, here we go again!

I. Writing Questions:

After reading this chapter, please go back to your annotations and write **three** WH-questions (questions that begin with what, when, where, who, which, how, how many, etc.), and **three** Yes/no questions (questions that begin with is, are, was, were, do, does, did, etc.).

WH-Questions:

1.

2.

3.

Yes/No Questions:

1.

2.

3.

- -

Discussion Question: Lin's love for music started at a young age when his mother used to listen to a radio station and sing along to Lin at the kitchen table. This inspired him to pursue a career in music compiling. Were you ever inspired by someone who has had a positive impact on your life or on any major decision you have made? Provide some examples for your answer.

II. VOCABULARY WORDS: Below, write the definition for each word, either by using context clues, or by looking them up in the dictionary.

1. dozen	9. determined	16. temporary
2. fond	10. overcome	17. energize
3. skyscraper	11. comprehensive	18. humanly
4. innovation	12. guide	19. remarkably
5. compile	13. individual	20. folk
6. devoted	14. contemporary	
7. audience	15. discourage	
8. fierce		

III. Use five new words from the table above to write an original sentence for each word.

1.

2.

3.

4.

5.

IV. In the table below, identify the part of speech for each word.

Word	Part of Speech (noun, verb, adjective, or adverb)
1. overcome	( )
2. comprehensive	( )
3. guide	( )
4. individual	( )
5. determined	( )
6. energized	( )
7. devoted	( )
8. fierce	( )
9. contemporary	( )
10. remarkably	( )

V. Internet Search: Do a search on the connection between music and mathematics. Then, write a short paragraph using your own words to explain to your classmates what you learned.

Zumurruda from Cairo, Egypt:
Still Dreaming

Thinking back to my childhood, the clear and vivid memories that come to my head are those I experienced on our small farm in a **rural** town called, Aswan, in Southern Cairo, Egypt. Our town sat directly on the Nile, a river that, according to many people, has been a life line for Egyptians for thousands of years because its water has been used for drinking, **irrigation** of plantations, and also for feluccas (Egyptian sail boats), which used to transport people to towns along the Nile river. Many dhows (vessels) also went up and down the Nile. They were mostly used for trade and fishing.

So, as many towns that were built around the Nile banks, Aswan benefited a great deal from the river. If you had a bird's eye view of Aswan, you would see that it is surrounded with cultivated land and animal farms. Compared to many farms around our area, ours was very small.

My father inherited this piece of land from his father, who also inherited it from his father, and it goes back many generations. My father says that the farm was much bigger at some point, but over the years, people around him, mostly uncles and aunts, kept taking a yard here and a yard there, and very soon, he was left with only a couple of acres.

As far back as I can remember, we were very poor. I had nine brothers and sisters, and my parents were always **struggling** to provide enough food for all of us, let alone other necessities or conveniences.

"We may not have much in this family but working hard will **pay off** in the end when you all get an education. Knowledge is the solution to come out of bad situations." These words were always repeated by my father.

My parents would always wake up very early in the morning and work till the late evening.

"We want you all to have what we did not have the chance to get. We want you to go to good schools and **obtain** degrees because this is the only way to escape **poverty**." My parents **engrained** this in our heads.

The walk to our school took about an hour, and sometimes when I walked to school with my brothers and sisters in the rain, we would be all wet and cold. We did not even own jackets or raincoats.

I remember sitting in class one morning and was shaking uncontrollably. My teeth were **chattering**. The teacher told me to stop shaking and pay attention to the lesson. The classrooms did have a heating system. So, we basically had to wear many layers of clothing to be able to **withstand** the freezing classrooms. It was even worse when were released for **recess**.

*"Why doesn't the teacher care that I was cold and wet? Why would the school not offer me some help and get me another shirt? Why would they want to see a **suffering** child and not do something about it?"* I wondered.

I was only eight years old. I knew even at that age that if I saw one of my friends in the same situation, I would try to help in any way I could. In fact, one time, I took off my shirt and put it on the baby lamb because he was **shivering** in the **stable**. His mother was very sick and was placed in a different corner of the stable.

Getting through the school day used to be a huge challenge for most of us, as many families around our school were as poor as we were, and maybe worse. For me and my siblings, the challenge did not end when we came home from school. Whether or not there was food, we had to sit and do our homework first.

We had other **obligations** and **chores** around the house, like feeding our **domestic** animals, such as cows and sheep and clean around the stable every day. We also needed to help clean the house, do the dishes, wash our clothes by hand and lay them out to dry. In addition, if anything else needed repair around the farm or the house, we had to help my father.

Some nights I would sit in the dark in a corner of a room that my nine brothers and sisters shared and would imagine myself to be a very successful business woman. I was always excellent in math. I wanted to use my skills to make money and help other people do the same. I mostly wanted to make my parents proud.

So, I would imagine buying a big beautiful house for them, and some nice cars. My older sister would yell at me and tell me to put my head on the pillow and go to sleep.

"Why are you always thinking about something? I see you every night just sitting there in the corner, staring at the window." She would ask.

I did not care. Even when I pretended to be asleep, I was still dreaming about the future.

Recalling these memories now sometimes upsets me, but they mostly motivate and encourage me to keep going and move forward. Those challenges that I had as a child have actually worked to my advantage, I think. When I used to see my parents struggling to **make ends meet**, it motivated me to work harder and improve my skills. I had promised my parents to always be a good student and strive for excellence in anything I did. So, I always tried to do just that.

Three years ago, my husband, our two children and I moved to the USA in hopes of finding a better life for us and a brighter future for our kids. I used to hear people back home say that in America, anyone can do well if they worked hard and followed the law, but in our case, it has been very tough. I cannot get a good job because I need to care for the children. I also go to school full-time, and I need to take care of everything else in the house. So, whenever I can find and accept a job, it is always part-time, and the pay is very low. If I do not have the necessary language skills in this country, I will have to continue accepting these jobs until I can get some kind of a degree.

I have been studying at a local community college for the last two years, and I am on the Honors list every semester. I want to keep my promise to myself, to my parents and to my husband. I also want to be a good role model for my children. I know they do not understand much right now, but they will, soon enough.

My husband has been trying to help as much as he can, but also, the low-paying job that he has, working in a mini market for a friend, has not been enough to pay for child care and house expenses. Even though he received a B.S. degree in Engineering back in Egypt, he cannot use this degree to get a good-paying job here. He also has to start from zero because his degree is not accepted in the U.S.A., and his English language skills are not very good.

When I see my husband working very hard and coming home extremely tired and unhappy, it really pushes and **urges** me even more to continue my education **despite** the fact that I am **exhausted** at the end of the day. Also, when I think about how little time I get to spend with my children during the day, it motivates me to finish school faster and start looking for a good job, which will hopefully offer me and my family some health benefits.

Since I did not have the chance to go to college in my country, I have found the opportunity here in California. I am very lucky to have this chance, as my other brothers and sisters still cannot go to college. I feel this is all on me now to finish and be financially successful. I will be the first person in my family to go to college and graduate. Everyone in my family, here and in Cairo is counting on me to get them out of poverty, and I will not rest until I make this happen.

My goal now is to get my AA degree and transfer to a university as a business major. Hopefully, I will also have the opportunity to get a master's degree in business. Then, my husband would like to go back to college and get an engineering degree so that we can start focusing on our children's education and **gradually** improve our standard of living.

I. Writing Questions:

After reading this chapter, please go back to your annotations and write **three** WH-questions (questions that begin with what, when, where, who, which, how, how many, etc.), and **three** Yes/no questions (questions that begin with is, are, was, were, do, does, did, etc.).

WH-Questions:

1.

2.

3.

Yes/No Questions:

1.

2.

3.

Discussion Question: In this story, Zumurruda is constantly dreaming and thinks she has to be the one person in the family to save everyone from poverty. Do you think her dreams are achievable in her situation? Do you think she is reasonable in taking on the responsibility of saving the whole family by herself? Provide support for your answer.

II. VOCABULARY WORDS: Below, write the definition for each word, either by using context clues, or by looking them up in the dictionary.

1. rural	8. recess	15. make ends meet
2. struggle	9. suffer	16. urge
3. pay off	10. shiver	17. despite
4. obtain	11. stable	18. exhausted
5. poverty	12. obligation	19. gradually
6. chatter	13. chore	
7. withstand	14. domestic	

III. Use five new words from the table above to write an original sentence for each word.

1.

2.

3.

4.

5.

IV. In the table below, identify the part of speech for each word.

Word	Part of Speech (noun, verb, adjective, or adverb)
1. urge	( )
2. exhausted	( )
3. gradually	( )
4. hesitate	( )
5. domestic	( )
6. obligation	( )
7. obtain	( )
8. poverty	( )
9. chatter	( )
10. rural	( )

V. Internet Search: Do a search on the equivalency of foreign college degrees. Then, write a short paragraph using your own words to explain to your classmates what you have learned about this topic. Give some names of online agencies that handle these equivalencies.

Printed in the United States
By Bookmasters